Sophomore

Sophomore

Breaking the Cycle

L.M. Spacek

Copyright © 2008 by L.M. Spacek.

ISBN: Softcover   978-1-4363-2514-1

All rights reserved. No part of this book may be reproduced or transmitted in any form or by any means, electronic or mechanical, including photocopying, recording, or by any information storage and retrieval system, without permission in writing from the copyright owner.

This is a work of fiction. Names, characters, places and incidents either are the product of the author's imagination or are used fictitiously, and any resemblance to any actual persons, living or dead, events, or locales is entirely coincidental.

This book was printed in the United States of America.

To order additional copies of this book, contact:
Xlibris Corporation
1-888-795-4274
www.Xlibris.com
Orders@Xlibris.com

"You learn when you get knocked down to get back up and go again. The tough will make it."

—Woody Hayes

Chapter 1

May 21

Kevin Humphries passes me the baton as he shouts, "GO, Billy! GO!"

I settle in behind the runner from Dayton Dunbar. Finding my stride, I zero in on the back of his yellow and green uniform. My spikes dig into the rubber track as I lean into the first turn. Into the shadows from the bleachers, around the second turn at the far end of the stadium, all I can hear is the pounding of feet into the track. That second turn is a lonely place. Around the 300 meter mark, my lungs feel like they're going to explode. But one thing I've learned is to never quit—never let your teammates down. Instead, I push through the pain, grunt, and start my kick. I can hear the breath of the other runner as I pass him on the straightaway and hand off the baton to Woody Fletcher.

Kevin gives me a high five and says, "Way to go, man."

I bend down with hands on knees to catch my breath. I've done my job. Less than fifty-five seconds later, Woody crosses the finish line with the baton raised in celebration. We win the relay and the meet.

I'm Billy Morris, the third leg in the 4 X 400 meter relay for the Cedarville High School Comets. Even though I'm only a freshman, I have the fourth fastest 400 meter time. The quarter mile could be the toughest race in track, and in every single meet, I have to run it twice, once in the open 400 and once in the 4 x 400 relay. The 400 lets you know how tough you are because around the 300 meter mark, you want to quit. Your legs feel like they're on fire. And that's how you feel when you're in shape.

Today was our last track meet. I like track, but I'm glad it's over. Now I can start to focus on the upcoming football season. In Cedarville, everyone goes to the football game on Friday night. The whole town packs the stadium. It's like a complete madhouse. In this town, football is a way of life.

When the meet is over, I walk across the campus to catch the last few innings of my best friend's baseball game. Jack Thompson is also only a freshman, but he's the starting pitcher on the varsity baseball team. He throws in the high 70's, low 80's, and he throws a slider. He calls it the Jack Thompson special. I swear the bottom just freaking drops out of that pitch. He makes most batters look stupid. Not only is Jack a great pitcher, but he can hit the hell out of the ball. When I climb to the top row of the bleachers, I see Jack in the batter's box. I know it's him because his curly brown hair sticks out from under his batting helmet. He has a man on second.

Jack's dad, Mr. Thompson, yells from just behind the fence on the first base side. His fingers shake the fence as he shouts, "Come on. Give it a ride. Show 'em what you got."

When Jack takes the first pitch for a strike, he steps out of the batter's box and turns toward the third base coach. Jack's jaw tightens as he hits the dirt from the bottom of his cleats with his bat. I can see the frustration on Jack's face as his dad continues shouting from behind the fence.

The other parents have moved away from Mr. Thompson, who strokes his mustache and fixes his worn out mechanic's hat that rests on top of his bald head. His white undershirt exposes his wiry frame and Popeye-like forearms. His arms are covered in tattoos. His Marine Corps tattoo is in plain view on his upper left arm. It's the one with the bulldog wearing the drill sergeant hat.

Jack's eyes narrow as he steps back into the batter's box. The pitcher delivers a hanging curve ball. Jack crushes it to left field. It's a line shot, but it just keeps carrying, like it has taken flight, clearing the fence by twenty feet.

The students and parents jump to their feet and go crazy, cheering and clapping. Jack rounds the bases and steps on home plate where he is mobbed by the entire team.

Cedarville takes the lead 4 to 3.

Mr. Thompson shouts, "That's my boy. How 'bout that!" As he turns from the fence and pumps his fist in the air, his shin catches the bottom row of the bleachers, and he stumbles and falls to the ground.

In the stands, Mr. Towers pulls out a cell phone and says, "I've seen enough. I'm calling the police. How many times is that guy going to show up drunk?"

Mr. Thompson picks himself up, looks around, and brushes off his oil-stained jeans. A huge cloud of dust surrounds him, and he repositions himself along the fence as the next batter swings at a high fastball and flies out to left field to end the inning.

Jack jogs out to the mound to close out the game. He adjusts his hat over his curly brown mop, and he pounds the ball into his glove.

Mr. Thompson shouts from behind the fence, "Let's go! Shut 'em down! Throw 'em the heat!"

The first batter steps up to the plate. Jack throws him a change up. The batter swings and pops it up behind home plate. The catcher moves under it and makes the catch. One out. Jack strikes out the next batter on three straight pitches. The first two pitches are fastballs. The third pitch is a nasty Jack Thompson special that the batter swings at and misses. Two outs.

Mr. Thompson's voice echoes through the stadium. "Look at my boy. Come on, son."

Jack's face gets more and more tense as his dad continues to yell. His next three pitches miss the strike zone. Then he throws a wild pitch in the dirt that skips past the catcher and crashes into the backstop, rattling the fence. He walks the next two batters.

Mr. Thompson roars from behind the fence, "What the hell! Come on ump! Ain't nothing wrong with them pitches! Open your eyes! You're costing us the game!"

The next batter hits a scorching grounder to shortstop Danny Towers, who barely knocks it down and makes a late throw to first base. The runner beats out the throw by half a step. The umpire flaps his arms out to the side and shouts, "Safe, Safe." The bases are loaded.

Mr. Thompson goes crazy, "He was out by a mile. You guys are blind." A Cedarville police cruiser rolls up in the parking lot. Mr. Thompson turns and notices the car, but he doesn't stop. "Let's go ump! Get in the game!"

Two officers climb out of their police cruiser and come up behind Jack's dad. Officer Polansky is short and skinny, and Officer Henning looks like a husky professional wrestler. They look like David Spade and Chris Farley, but everyone knows this isn't funny. The officers approach Mr. Thompson, and the crowd's attention shifts from the game to the scene behind the fence on the first base side. Jack looks over at his father and the two police officers. Mr. Thompson knows the routine. He is led away from the field and guided into the back of the cruiser.

Cedarville's head baseball coach, Coach Logan, jogs out to the mound and says some words to Jack, pats him on the back, and returns to the dugout. Jack's next three pitches are fast balls filled with rage, probably 82 or 83 miles per hour. The dust explodes from the catcher's mitt on each pitch. The batter swings and misses all three: game over.

The players from both teams walk out onto the infield and shake hands. It's a mixture of the royal blue and gold from Cedarville and the light blue and gray of Tipp City. Jack grabs his glove and bat-bag and walks toward me.

"Great game, bro," I say, raising my fist for a fist bump.

"Thanks." Jack responds by half-heartedly hitting my fist.

"I think that home run you crushed is still going."

He forces a smile. "The guy threw me a hanger."

We continue to walk back toward the school. I look over at Jack, "What about your old man?"

"He embarrasses the hell out of me." Jack kicks a stone out in front of us.

"What can you do?"

"I don't know. I tell him not to come," Jack says.

"Well, at least baseball's over," I say, trying to make my best friend feel better.

"Yeah, but then it starts all over again with football season." As we walk across the track on our way back to the school, Jack stops and looks over at me. "You know something?" Jack looks back at the baseball field where his father was just taken away by the police. "Sometimes . . . I wish he was dead."

Chapter 2

June 9th

I stare at Cindy. Her bleached-blonde hair contrasts with her year-round tan. I'm convinced that I am the luckiest kid in school. Her bright green t-shirt has a yellow lemon on the front. It reads: **Squeeze ME!!** And that's exactly what I want to do. I'm so into her that when I'm around her it's hard for me to form a complete sentence. I feel like an idiot. She just transferred to Cedarville from Nashville, Tennessee at the beginning of our freshman year. Her dad was hired as the high school math teacher and the head swimming coach.

She notices me staring, and she pushes her long blonde hair behind her ears. "Billeee," she says in her Southern drawl, "would y'all pay attention. If y'all don't pass this final, you won't to be able to play ball next year. Mr. Handler told you that you needed to pass this test, or y'all are in danger of failing English."

"I already looked over the study guide a hundred times. I'll be fine." This is actually the first test I studied for all year.

Our ninth grade English teacher at Cedarville, Mr. Handler, made Cindy my study partner. I think he was playing matchmaker. Lucky for me, I didn't get Joey Fineman as a partner, that dude teaches computer programming classes to adults. Instead, I got Cindy Landry. Seriously, she has it all: big green eyes, blonde hair, and with all the swimming that she does, well, let's just say she's in great shape.

We've been hanging out for almost three months.

On my way to her DVD collection, I push her on the shoulder because I want to touch her. "C'mon, let's just hang out and watch a movie." I look through her collection. "Hey, how about *Billy Madison?*"

Cindy shakes her head. "Would y'all stop screwing around? This test is important. Y'all need a good grade." Cindy's on the honor roll, and she was the captain of the freshman cheerleading squad.

If it weren't for Cindy, English class would be unbearable. Forty-five minutes of English with Mr. Handler seems like an eternity. I usually sit in the back of the class and draw pictures of football players and practice writing my autograph so it will be perfect when I become a professional running back in the NFL. I wouldn't even be studying for this test if Mr. Handler hadn't explained to me that I needed to pass it in order to be eligible for football next year.

I move around the basement shooting pool and playing air-hockey. As she quizzes me, I stroll past her and poke her because it is impossible for me to keep my hands off her.

While painting her finger nails some fluorescent pink color, which happens to match the color of her toe nails, Cindy goes through about twenty questions. She covers everything from John Steinbeck's *Of Mice and Men* to J.D. Salinger's *Catcher in the Rye*. When we finally finish the study guide she asks, "Are y'all sure yer going to be okay on the test?"

I roll my eyes. "I knew all those questions, didn't I? I'll be fine."

She looks at her watch. "Shouldn't yew call your mom and tell her y'all are still here? It's getting late."

"I doubt she cares. She's probably with her new boyfriend."

"Why are yew so hard on her? Y'all know she loves yew." I hate when Cindy is right, which is pretty much all the time.

"I guess it's because my dad's not around to blame." Mom never really filled me in on the details as to why she and my dad got divorced. My old man just kind of disappeared, took a new position with his company and moved to California, about 2,000 miles away from Dayton, which seems to be just fine with my mom. He sends me birthday cards and says things like, "How's it going, champ?"

Cindy applies some more nail polish. "Y'all can't go on blaming her forever."

I line up the cue ball and sink the eight ball in the side pocket. "Yeah, I know."

"Listen, even if y'all don't call yer mom, yew still have to go. My dad says 'no boys after ten'," Cindy says while guiding me up the steps to the front door. Did I mention that I love when she touches me?

We walk upstairs from the basement. Mrs. Landry, a stay-at-home mom, sits on their brown leather sofa. Her short brown hair turns up at her shoulders. Mr. Landry is next to her. They are watching a Seinfeld rerun.

I poke my head into the living room and wave. "Goodnight," I say.

"Oh, goodnight, Billy," they respond almost in unison, looking up from their sitcom. I swear Cindy has the All-American family.

Cindy walks outside with me and closes the door. "Thanks for coming over," she says as she takes my hand. She looks toward the ground in a shy way. I love that about her.

"Yeah, thanks for helping me study."

"I'll see y'all tomorrow?"

"Yeah, tomorrow." Despite the fact that we've been hanging out for three months, things are still awkward between us. She finally leans in for a kiss. I kiss her back. Her lips are soft. I get dizzy, and my face turns red.

She turns and heads back to her house. I look at the back of her shorts that read: **Go Comets!** I get on my beat-up, rusted out, royal blue dirt bike, the Exploder, my crappy means of transportation, and pedal down the road. Cindy's house is only a few miles away from mine.

On the way home and just because it's on the way, I stop by Jack's house. All the lights are on, so I jump off the Exploder and walk up the driveway. As I get closer to their front porch, I hear shouting coming from an open window. I hear the voices of Mr. and Mrs. Thompson.

"When are you going get a job?" she shouts.

"Get off my back!" Mr. Thompson's voice echoes from the house. I can feel his voice in my bones.

She persists, "All you do is sit on that couch and drink." The television blares the 10 o'clock news in the background.

Jack interrupts, "Mom, just let it go."

"No, I'm not done. He just sits here everyday feeling sorry for himself, drinking until he can't see straight."

Mr. Thompson growls in his scratchy voice, "I work! Been working on the cars in the garage. I'm just about finished rebuilding that 57 Chevy. It'll sell at the car show."

Mrs. Thompson shouts, "You've been saying that for two years!"

I hear a door slam, and the yelling stops. I jump on my bike and start home. Pedaling down the dimly lit street, I think about Jack's life. As I pass the single street lamp, my bike casts a giant shadow. I wonder how Jack deals with his dad. Sometimes I get upset that my dad isn't around. But if having him around meant living like Jack, I guess I'm better off. But sometimes I miss my dad, wish he was around, wish we shared the time other kids share with their dad's: play catch in the yard, go for bike rides, do the things dads and sons are supposed to do. I cut through our neighbor's backyard where our back porch light is on. I pull around to the front of the house and park my bike in the garage.

As soon as I walk into the mudroom, my mom calls from the kitchen.

"Where have you been? It's almost 11." She just got off her shift as line manager at the Mead Paper Company.

"Cindy's."

"Would you please come here?"

Annoyed, I look up from the bottom of the kitchen steps. "What?"

She drinks from a cup of coffee and reads the newspaper, trying to unwind after her shift. She looks over the top of the newspaper. "Why are you home so late?"

"I was studying for my last final," I say this like I have a million things to do.

"I'm not mad, I just want to know. You know, the minute you get home, you walk down those steps and disappear into that basement, that dungeon. I want to know how you are. I miss you." My mom sets down the newspaper and runs her fingers through her hair, a sign that she is stressed. The communication between us since my dad left has almost completely shut down.

"I'm fine. School's fine," I say, as I walk down the steps to my room. I flip on the light. My room is covered in posters. LeBron James is on one wall. My Ray Lewis poster has him doing that crazy dance when he comes out of the tunnel onto the field. The Ken Griffey Jr. poster holds some of my medals and ribbons from middle school track meets. I have a cool Dave Matthew's Band poster and a custom made neon light that I got from my dad before he moved out. In red and blue letters it shines: Billy's Place.

I brush my teeth and take out my contacts. I set my alarm, turn off my light, and climb into bed. As I lie in bed, I think about what Cindy said about forgiving my mom for the divorce. I think about my dad 2,000 miles away. And I think about my best friend and what he has to deal with. My CD player spins the Dave Matthew's song *Stay or Leave*, and I fall asleep.

Chapter 3

June 10th

The next morning, I wake up early, at six a.m. I look over my notes one last time. This is a test I know I have to pass. If I fail the test, I fail English, and that would make me ineligible for football. Which just happens to be *the* most important thing in my life. My exam isn't until nine a.m., and it's the last test of my freshman year of high school.

I jump in the shower, throw on my favorite Ohio State Buckeye's shorts and my blue and gold Cedarville football shirt that boasts: Pain is Temporary, Pride is Forever. I put on my tattered Cincinnati Red's hat, grab my backpack, jump on the Exploder, and ride to school. In the center of town, the main street is lined with stores. Mr. Stams owns the Cedarville market and grocery store. They have the best rhubarb pies, and I work there part time in the summer. On the corner is Mills' diner where everyone hangs out. It's the best place in Cedarville to get a burger and fries. There's the local post office and Mrs. Mastadon's dress shop. The center of town is a perfect square, and in the center of that square is a little park with perfectly cut grass. Sometimes in the summer, folk or jazz bands play in the ivory white gazebo. Cedarville is not a very wealthy town, but the people here take great pride in it.

Just north of town is Cedarville High School. Friday nights in the fall, this side of town is lit up. The people of Cedarville not only take great pride in their town, they take great pride in their football team. I jump off my bike and head to my English class for my last exam. Walking through the halls, I call to Jack and my buddy Tombo. "What's up, fellas?"

"Hey, Billy. What's up, bro?" Tombo asks leaning against the row of dark gray lockers.

"Hanging in there man, only one more day," I say, adjusting my hat.

"Dude, check out my new shirt." Tombo, who is a 5'9" fireplug and has no neck, spins around and shows off his new shirt. It's black with red skulls, which is much different than his old shirt, the red one with black skulls. He's an idiot, but I love him.

I see Cindy standing by her locker. When I get close to her, I smell her Alfred Sung perfume. It drives me crazy. "Y'all ready for the test?" she asks.

"Yeah. You?"

"Of course!"

In the classroom, Mr. Handler pulls a pen from the pocket protector of his white, short-sleeved dress shirt. He looks through his coke-bottle glasses over a piece of paper, passes out the tests and blue books, and fixes the few strands of hair that try desperately to cover his bald head. He says, "Good luck everyone. When you're finished with the exam, put it on my desk, and you're free to go. Have a great summer!"

I open the exam like I'm in a NASCAR race. I can't wait to get it over with. The test is filled with questions from the study guide. There are questions about Shakespeare's *Romeo and Juliet*, but I saw the movie with Leonardo DiCaprio, so I'm good there. There are questions about *Mary Shelley's Frankenstein*. Saw that one too; the one where Robert De Niro plays the monster and Kenneth Branagh plays Dr. Frankenstein. It's actually not a bad flick. I know I did well. I've never studied harder for anything in my life. But seriously, who needs English class when Tombo's mom has just about every movie ever made? I shoot Mr. Handler a smile as I hand in my exam and step out into the hallway. I'm sure he hates me.

Jack strolls down the hall with his newest girlfriend, Leigh Hautman. I can't figure out what Jack sees in her. She's like this dark gothic figure. She has a bar pierced through her eyebrow, and she wears black fingernail polish. Her hair is jet black, and she wears this heavy mascara that makes her eyes seem like tiny black holes. Maybe he likes her because she's a junior and older, and she drives this old, light blue, beat up Dodge Charger that her brother fixed up for her. Her brother is in the Vocational Ed program. She drives us everywhere.

"Hey, who's finished with school this year? No longer a freshman," I shout out.

"I guess you are," Jack replies, his curly hair trying to explode from under his royal blue Cedarville baseball hat.

"What are you up to?" I ask.

"Leigh and I are going to get some food. Want to go?"

"No man, I'm going to the weight room. Coach wants us to start summer lifting today. I swear that guy's crazy."

"What do you expect? If he didn't blow out his knee at Notre Dame, he'd be playing on Sundays," Jack responds.

"Well, whatever, I'm starting now, and so should you."

"I'll catch up with you."

Leigh barely even looks at me, turns her head and gives me a half wave.

In the weight room, I am met by, not surprisingly, Coach Murphy. I think that dude lives there. He's a freaking monster, 6' 4" with broad shoulders, wavy blond hair, unshaven, as always. He's got a huge wad of smelly chewing tobacco in his mouth, and even though he's only a few feet away from me, he shouts like he's on the other end of a football field, "Glad you could make it, Mr. Morris." He spits his tobacco into a clear plastic cup and slaps me on the back. His innocent slap sends my whole body lunging two feet forward. "Let's get you going," he says, as he grabs my folder. It has a daily workout schedule. Six days a week. Weights on Monday, Wednesday, and Friday. Conditioning on Tuesday, Thursday, and Saturday. "No rest for the wicked," he grunts. Then he gets this mischievous grin. "Mr. Morris, today I will be your personal trainer."

As he directs me to the squat rack, I think to myself, how did I get into this mess?

I step under the bar and lift it off the rack. He stands behind me and yells, "Let's go, son!" In the mirror that covers the entire sidewall, I catch the other guys from the team looking over, shaking their heads and laughing, elbowing each other and pointing at me. They are glad they are not in my shoes.

Coach Murphy shouts in between reps. "You want to start, you gotta man up." We go from machine to machine and work out repetition after repetition. I do preacher curls until I can't bend my arms, or straighten them. One hour and twenty different exercises later, I can't even stand up without feeling like I'm going to puke.

The spit and tobacco in Coach Murphy's plastic cup adds to my nausea. He sees I'm almost dead and jokes, "Morris, we'll skip the plyometrics today." Because I have done so many squats, each step I take is painful. I have done so many military presses that I can't raise my hands above my shoulders. After thirty minutes of lying on the leg press machine, I steady myself and stagger outside to my bike. I say every bad word that I know realizing that I have about a three mile ride home. I'm about to try to pick up my bike and just throw it in the dumpster when I see Jack and Leigh driving up in her beat-up Dodge Charger.

"You all right, bro?" Jack asks. I must look as pale as a ghost.

"I'm not sure," I mutter back, "I just got put through the Murphy workout from hell."

Jack glances over at Leigh. "Yeah, I'll take him home," she says.

Jack says, "I'll bring your bike to your house when I'm done." As he heads off to the weight room, I ease myself into Leigh's car. A skull and crossbones key chain hangs from her rearview mirror. I sink into the soft cloth seats.

"You doing okay?" Leigh asks.

"Yeah, I'll be fine. I just gotta lie down."

Her black painted nails work the five-speed, and my whole body can feel every time the car shifts gears. Her wrists are covered in rubber bracelets. Her yellow Live Strong bracelet sticks out between all the other dark blue and black ones. We speed through the town, going way over the speed limit, barely missing a gray Honda Civic as it turns onto a side street. She looks directly at me. While downshifting she says, "You know, the whole world is based on timing."

My head spins and my stomach kills. She blasts this heavy, punk rock, and I feel like I'm in some strange version of hell.

When we stop in my driveway, I ease myself out of the passenger seat.

"Thanks for the ride," I say.

"No problem."

Because my arms are still killing me, I have trouble pulling open the front door. I walk in the house and ease myself down the basement steps to my bedroom, fall face first on my bed, and crash for two hours.

When I wake up, my body aches all over. I splash some water on my face and look at myself in the mirror. My spiked brown hair is sticking straight up, and my hazel eyes squint back. Brushing my teeth that were just recently freed from the braces I wore for two years, I lean into the mirror with my hand on the sink.

Jack dropped off the Exploder after his workout, so I jump on the bike and ride over to Cindy's house. When I knock on the front door, no one answers, so I walk around to her backyard. Cindy is floating on a raft in their pool, wearing a bright yellow bikini.

"Come on in! The water's perfect," she calls from the pool.

I throw a raft in the water and jump in. The cool water washes over me and my sore muscles. We float around the pool enjoying the fact that summer is finally here, a summer that would change my life . . . forever.

Chapter 4

June 11ᵗʰ First day of Summer

The next morning, I roll out of bed and hit the play button on my CD player. The Dave Matthew's Band fires off *Don't Drink the Water*. I start my day with fifty push-ups and one hundred sit-ups. After yesterday's workout, everything aches, but once I get started, I loosen up. I run my regular two-mile route, up and down the hills of my neighborhood. It's still early, so it's quiet, except for the few people in their pajamas getting their morning paper. The sun is coming up, and there's not a cloud in the sky. After my jog, I jump on the Exploder, and start pedaling toward the track.

When I get just outside the track, I see someone running down the bleacher steps. I squint, trying to get a better view. When I get close enough, I'm surprised to see that Jack is already there and ready to run a workout. "What's up?" Jack says.

"What are you doing here so early?" I ask.

Jack looks away like he's searching for the answer up in the stands that surround the stadium. "If I'm out of the house before my dad wakes up, I don't have to deal with him."

"C'mon, a good workout will take your mind off things."

Jack nods his head. "Good idea."

We start with four 100 meter strides. Then we run our eight 200 hundred meter sprints. The sun beats down, starting to tan our winter-white skin. We get into the grind, the hard work. We run the bleachers, up and down, up and down. The truth is, I love it. I love finding out just how hard I can push myself. It's good that Jack is here. I can push him, and he makes me work harder. We end the workout with a light two lap cool down. Summer will be long, but we know the hard work will pay off.

As we come to the end of our cool down, I ask, "What are you up to tonight?"

"Leigh and I are going to the drive-in. You and Cindy want to go?"

"Yeah, sure, we'll go. What's playing?" I ask.

"I think *Goldmember*, with Austin Powers and Dr. Evil."

"Dude, that's perfect. Can you guys pick us up at six?"

Jack laughs as he raises his pinky finger to his mouth and gives his best Dr. Evil impression. "Yeah, for one *million* dollars."

I give him a push on the back and say, "Good workout today." I pause for a second and continue, "Don't worry about that stuff with your dad. It'll get better."

* * *

Jack and Leigh pull in my driveway a little bit after six.

Cindy and I climb into the back of the Charger. We all start talking at once during the ride to the drive-in. Even though Leigh and Cindy are very different, they get along. I guess it's one of the cool things about Cedarville, most of the kids at our school seem to get along.

"You doing anything fun over the summer?" Leigh asks Cindy.

"Lake Michigan, my family goes there every summer. What do you have planned this summer?" Cindy asks Leigh from the back seat.

Even though she is asking Leigh, I jump in. "After working out this summer, Jack and I are going to be the starting backfield on the varsity football team. We're going to win Cedarville a State Championship."

Cindy rolls her eyes. "Y'all think Coach Murphy will start two sophomores?"

"If he's smart he will," I add.

Cindy asks, "What about yew Leigh? What are y'all doing this summer?"

"I'm going to this cool music festival in July to party with my friends. I can't wait for my senior year." Leigh says, as she pulls into the drive-in.

During the movie, I get close to Cindy in the back of Leigh's Dodge Charger. During the scene where Austin Powers meets Goldmember at the disco club, I put my arm around her and rub the back of her neck. At this point, Jack and Leigh are going at it, I mean tongue and all. Cindy and I look at each other.

I finally say, "Hey you guys, we're going for a walk."

Jack and Leigh don't even stop making out. Jack simply raises his hand and waves goodbye. Cindy and I slide out the door to watch the end of the movie in the back of the park on a bench. I put my arm around her and pull her close. She runs her fingers through my hair and leans into me. She whispers in my ear, "Billy, I think I love yew."

I almost fall off the bench. "What?" I ask.

She gets a look on her face that shows she wishes she could take all those words back. "I just really like being with yew."

This is new territory for me. I look at her and because I don't know what to say, I mutter, "I like hanging out with you."

For the last fifteen minutes of the movie, we sit in an awkward silence, occasionally exchanging an uncomfortable glance.

When the movie ends, we walk back to meet up with Jack and Leigh. Turns out, Austin Powers and Dr. Evil are really brothers. Who knew?

* * *

On the 4th of July, Cindy, Leigh, Jack, and I go to the Cedarville Park, where the city is having its annual Home Days Carnival. The Ferris wheel goes around and around, the lights on the rides blink like crazy, and everyone gets their fill of cotton candy, corn dogs, and fresh squeezed lemonade.

The four of us walk around from one game to another, checking out all the different things to do. At one of the booths, a giant man covered in tattoos yells out, "Four balls for a dollah. Knock down all four tahgets and win a prize."

I want to impress Cindy, so I open my wallet and pull out a few bucks.

The dude exposes his yellow teeth. Three are missing. "One dollah fuh' foah baseballs. You gotta knock down all foah tahgets to win." He raises his eyebrows as if to say . . . *suckahs*.

I turn to Jack and quote Austin Powers in my best British accent, "Carnies, circus folk, small hands, smell like cabbage." Determined, I hand the carnie a dollar bill. Five dollars and four tries later, I win Cindy a five-foot panda bear. The tattooed man hands over the bear.

I give the bear to Cindy, and she gives it a big hug. "Thanks," she says. "Y'all were awesome."

"No problem," I say proudly.

As the sun starts to go down, we head over to the baseball fields to watch the fireworks, and we grab a couple blankets from Leigh's car on the way. We find an open area in the outfield where we unfold our blankets, and we sit in a half circle to face the fireworks. The first few fireworks get *oohs* and *ahhs* from the crowd. The reds and blues sparkle in the blackness. Moms and Dads point their fingers into the night sky as the little kids look up with wonder. I ease my arm around Cindy feeling the warm skin on her lower back. My cold hands make her jump, but then she relaxes and melts into my arms.

The fireworks explode, and Bruce Springsteen's *Born in the U.S.A.*, and Neil Diamond's *Coming to America* blare through the speakers. Everything seems right with the world.

Chapter 5

July 7th

"Billy honey," my mom shouts from upstairs, "would you come here for a minute?"

This is usually not a good sign. I reluctantly make my way upstairs from the basement.

"What's up?" my mom asks, sitting in the corner of our light green sectional sofa.

"Nothing," I say looking down at her skeptically.

She sits up straight and takes a deep breath. It's a here-we-go deep breath. "You know, I've been thinking," she begins. This is also usually not a good sign.

"About what?" I ask cautiously.

"Well, ever since your dad and I got divorced, I've been thinking about getting out of Cedarville. You know, starting over."

I shift uncomfortably from one foot to the other. "What are you talking about?"

"Well, Richard and I have been talking about maybe moving, you know, somewhere warmer. He travels a lot, and most of his business is in South Carolina."

"No way, mom! This isn't fair!" I say becoming more defensive.

Richard is my mom's boyfriend. Because we don't get along, I call him Dick. His dark features and his close-set eyes can be intimidating. He claims he played linebacker for the Oklahoma Sooners. He's been to a few of my freshman football games, and he criticizes the hell out of me—pointing out every little mistake. I think time has made him believe he was one of the best college linebackers ever to play at Oklahoma. Time makes heroes out of all of us.

My mom says, "You know, I feel like I've spent most of my life at that factory."

"This isn't fair."

"I'll tell you what's not fair, me getting no help from your father and having to work twelve hours a day. That's what's not fair."

"There's no way I'm leaving Cedarville," I say in a more determined voice.

"Well, Richard suggested Bertram Academy. I think that might be a good idea."

"You want to send me to Bertram?" My legs feel like I've just done thirty reps on the squat rack.

My mom gives me this hope-filled look. "It's a good school. I want what's best for you."

"Cedarville's a good school."

"You haven't brought a book home all year."

I stumble, knowing that she's right. I can't even think of anything to say.

"Bertram will give you a chance to go to a good college." My mom gets up from the couch and moves toward me.

"I can get into a good college going to Cedarville."

"Bertram will give you a better chance. Richard has nothing but good things to say about it. He says Bertram has the best education around, and their sports teams are always competitive. He thinks you'd do great there."

"I bet he does. He probably just wants to get rid of me."

My mom moves right next to me. "You know, why can't you just get along with him?"

"He's never said one nice thing to me. Have you ever heard him after one of my football games?"

"Sometimes you are not the easiest person to get along with. Besides, he just wants to help." My mom goes to rub my back.

I avoid her touch. "He doesn't care about me." My heart pounds in my chest. I feel like I've been backed into a corner.

Our arguing is interrupted when the doorbell rings.

"That must be him." On her way to the door she looks over at me. "We're going to the movies, would you like to go?"

"I don't think so," I say like the answer is an obvious one.

She grabs her purse from the kitchen table, and before she goes to the front door she looks at me. "I wish you would give Richard a chance, and I want you to start thinking about Bertram."

As I storm past her on my way downstairs to my bedroom, I say, "There's no way I'm going to Bertram."

My mom gives me one of those we'll-see-about-that looks. "What are you going to do while we're gone?" my mom calls after me.

"PlayStation."

"Fine," my mom says from the top of the basement steps, letting out a deep sigh as our confrontation comes to an end. "I love you."

I close the door to my room, and I watch out my window as my mom and Dick drive away.

Chapter 6

July 9th to August 6th

Early on Wednesday morning, I walk out to the mailbox and find my report card in between junk mail and a bill from the electric company. Filled with apprehension, I slide open the yellow envelope that holds my grades from my freshman year and for my future. I check my final grades: Science: C, Math: B, Social Studies: D. I hold my breath when I get down to English. I remember to breathe when I see a D-. I passed—barely—but I passed.

Later that morning, Cindy calls me up.

"What's up?" I ask.

"I asked my mom if it was okay to invite yew to our lake house up in Michigan. She was cool with it. Can y'all believe that? It's the coolest place ever. What do yew think?" she asks.

"Are you kidding? That would be awesome!" I stop and think for a minute. "But, I'm not sure what my mom will say."

"Well, let me know if she says it's okay."

"I'll call you back!"

In the living room, my mom is watching her favorite soap opera, *Days of our Lives*. Because I don't initiate many conversations, she looks surprised. Also, because we haven't talked since our Bertram discussion, she knows that I want something. "Yeeeessss," she says in a what-do-you-want kind of way.

"Cindy and her family are going to her lake house in Michigan. I was wondering if I could go?"

"Are her parents okay with this?" My mother gives me a suspicious look.

"Her parents said it was fine."

"Where are you going to sleep?"

"In separate rooms."

She is quiet for a long time, and I can almost see the wheels spinning in her head. She asks, "When are they planning on leaving?"

"This Friday."

My mom waits for a long couple minutes and considers whether or not she should let her fifteen year old son spend a weekend with his girlfriend. I have to admit I am surprised when she finally says, "Yeah, okay. I think that would be all right."

"Seriously?" I say, feeling the excitement.

"Just make sure I get a phone number where I can reach you."

"Thanks mom!" I say, realizing that my mom is really pretty cool. And when I really think about it, I feel bad that we have drifted so far apart.

* * *

Friday morning, we hit the road in the Landry family van. It's a dark green Honda minivan. The drive is easy, maybe five hours with a few rest stops along the way. We navigate through some back roads to get to the place. A dirt driveway, lined with trees, winds all the way back to their cottage. It looks like a log cabin, but it has electricity and a fireplace. It smells like cedar and feels like a home. We unload the van and fill the refrigerator with food and unpack our luggage. Cindy shows me the upstairs of the cottage and the sleeper-couch in the loft, which is where I'll be sleeping. From my couch and through the window, I can see out over the lake. There are a few boats out on the water and not a cloud in the sky.

After we put our bags inside, Cindy and I head out to the back yard. I stop in my tracks seeing how awesome the lake really is. Cindy was right. It is the most beautiful place I've ever seen! The water is crystal clear. Standing on the dock, I can see all the way to the bottom of the lake.

"How long have you been coming here?" I ask.

"Since I was about five years old. My dad bought it from a friend. We got our boat used, but it works just fine."

I look around and see that they have a paddle boat, a canoe, and a ski boat. I am pumped.

That night we hang out with Cindy's parents and play Scrabble. I come in last place. I've never met a family that is so serious about playing Scrabble. Her mom scores 200 points, and her dad scores 150. Cindy has 135, and I finish with 70. And me, well, I feel like an idiot.

When the game is over, I say goodnight to Cindy and her family and head up to the loft. Because I can't sleep, I sit up for almost an hour staring at the ceiling as a cool breeze moves through my window. I think about Cindy, Jack, Leigh, football, and the beginning of my sophomore year. But it's mostly football that's on my mind; I've never looked forward to anything more in my life. The sound of the crickets comes through my window, as the water laps against the shore.

I wake up in the morning to a perfect view of the lake. The water sparkles like glass, and the sun peaks over the trees. It's like heaven on earth.

Cindy and I grab the canoe and paddle around the lake visiting the ducks. Trees line the shore, and the leaves are a bright green. The sun reflects off the water, a golden glow. Because we are up so early, we are just about the only people on the water, except for a few fishermen.

"I can't wait until this year starts," Cindy says, dipping her paddle in the water.

"Me too."

We glide around the lake. "It's going to be awesome," she says.

"Absolutely." I use my paddle to steer the canoe toward a nearby cove.

When we get into the cove, we stop paddling. Cindy smiles at me. "I mean, we got nothing holding us back."

I lean back on the end of the canoe and say, "I can't wait for football."

"I can't wait for cheerleading."

"It's gonna be great not to be freshman any more."

"Y'all are right about that."

"It's like we got the world at our fingertips."

When the canoe stops, Cindy steadies herself as she climbs over the middle bar of the canoe and sits next to me on the narrow seat. She puts her hand behind my neck, and looks me in the eye, and leans into me. Her lips are soft and wet.

I try to get closer to her, when suddenly, our weight shifts to one side, and before we know it, we are in the water, soaked! We look at each other and start laughing. She moves toward me and gives me a big hug as we plunge back into the water. We pull the canoe on shore and empty it out, laughing the entire time.

Back at the dock, Cindy's dad is waiting. I think we're in trouble, but he looks at our soaking wet clothes and rolls his eyes. "Are you guys ready?" he asks dangling the boat keys in his hand.

Cindy and I jump onto the dock and tie up the canoe. We help unsnap the boat cover.

Mr. Landry settles into the driver seat and turns the key in the ignition. He puts the boat in neutral and revs the engine. It rumbles to life.

We run up to the house to put on our swimsuits.

While walking back down to the boat, Cindy calls to her dad, "Can I do a dock start, Dad?"

"Let's do it."

She steps up on the dock, puts on a black ski vest, and wedges her feet into the double bindings of the ski. She grabs the wide blue handle of the yellow ski rope. Her dad puts the boat in gear as the slack in the rope tightens.

Mr. Landry yells from the boat, "Are you ready speed king?"

"Let her happen captain," she shouts back.

Mr. Landry puts the boat into gear, and Cindy slides into the water. She pulls back on the rope and is up almost immediately. As we drive to the other side of the lake, Cindy takes a couple of easy passes across the wake. When we get to the slalom course, she gives the thumbs up. Mr. Landry increases the speed to thirty-six miles per hour. Cindy cuts hard across the wake and goes around the first buoy, lying almost horizontal to the water. She races toward the next buoy, and she finishes the course without a miss. I am completely impressed.

Then it's my turn. As I prepare for my first time on skis in front of Cindy, Mr. Landry circles around to bring me the handle of the towrope. Sitting in the water, I think about skiing when I was little. Before my dad moved out, we would ski early on Saturday and Sunday mornings. We would arrive at six a.m. when the lake was flat. My dad loved flat water on a sunny August morning. "God's Country," he called the lake just outside of Cedarville. We would ski for three hours straight, each taking turns. Those are some of my favorite memories of growing up.

Mr. Landry shouts, "Let's get you going. You can do it."

I do my best on the slalom course, but not nearly as well as Cindy. I manage to catch the first two buoys and nearly kill myself when I wipe out trying to catch the third one.

Mr. Landry drives over. "Don't worry, by tomorrow you'll be going through that course like it's your job." When I'm with Cindy's family, it's one of the few times that I really think about the divorce of my parents and the things that I'm missing. Instead of having a great life at home with loving parents, I am stuck with my mom's boyfriend, ex-linebacker, Dick. Sometimes, I miss my dad.

Mr. Landry is a great teacher, and by Sunday afternoon, he has me running through the slalom course and catching at least four buoys. He seems to really be proud of me. He encourages me, "If you don't become a professional football player, you can always become a water skier." I can't remember the last time I felt so good about myself.

On the drive back to Cedarville, I consider the fact that I'll miss the canoe adventures, the roar of the ski boat, and just floating around Lake Michigan. I'm sad to leave, but I am completely energized when I think about football starting in one week.

Sitting in the back of the Landry van, I think back to the night at the movie theater when Cindy told me that she loved me. When I look over at Cindy, I think that I'm feeling the same way . . .

* * *

With one week of summer vacation left, I am stronger and faster. My five foot eleven inch frame is solid, chiseled from stone. I have worked harder than ever before for this football season.

Coach Murphy says that Jack and I have the best attendance record of any of the players. Jack even surprised me with how hard he's worked. He's in great shape. But now he's acting totally weird. He's got this new mean streak, doesn't have the same laid back personality. He doesn't laugh much, or even smile for that matter. And lately, he's always on edge.

At the end of one of our lifting workouts, I ask Jack, "What's going on with you?"

"Nothing," he fires back.

"Somebody piss you off?"

Jack looks me in the eye, hesitates.

"What's up?" I ask again.

"Nothing, I'm fine."

"You're totally not fine. You're my best friend. Don't you think I would know if you weren't fine? You haven't been right the last couple weeks."

And maybe it's because we're best friends that he comes clean. "My mom left. Last weekend, she just up and left."

My eyes widen. "Why?"

Jack looks down. "My parents got in a huge fight."

"What happened?"

"My dad was sitting on the couch, not doing anything, like usual. My mom asked him for like the hundredth time when he was going to get a job. He freaked out, said that finding work wasn't easy. My mom said he was lazy and good for nothing. My dad got up and pushed her across the room, and she hit her head on the side of the door. She was bleeding pretty bad. She dabbed her head with her hand and saw the blood. She got this terrified look on her face and ran upstairs to grab some of her stuff. Then she took off out the door."

"What'd you do?" I ask.

Jack takes a deep breath and collects himself. "So we got in my dad's car and went to the hospital looking for her, but she wasn't there. On the drive home from the hospital, my dad starts telling me it was my fault she left. He was blaming me. Can you believe that? Ever since he lost his job, he's been drinking everyday. Doesn't do a damn thing but work on those stupid cars in the garage. Can you believe he was blaming me?"

"We gotta do something."

"Yeah, what do you suggest?"

"I don't know." I look at my best friend who looks completely defeated. "We'll figure something out."

* * *

I stop by Jack's house during our last weekend of freedom before two-a-days. His mom still hasn't come home yet. As I near the house, I hear shouting coming from the kitchen.

Mr. Thompson yells, "You ain't nothing."

I look in through the side window and see Mr. Thompson pushing Jack in between sips from his Miller beer can. "You're just a loser. You ain't never going to amount to nothing." His wipes his hands on his grease-stained undershirt.

Jack just stands there, looking at his father, nodding his head.

"You're lazy." He pushes Jack in the chest.

Jack takes the hit.

"Why don't you try taking your old man? Come on, Alice."

When his dad calls him Alice, Jack moves back. These words pack more than a punch.

I've seen Jack destroy 220 pound fullbacks and punish 240 pound linebackers. He could have taken down his dad, destroyed him. What is it that doesn't allow us to fight an injustice when it comes from our own family?

Jack continues to back up as his father moves toward him.

"Come on, tough guy," Mr. Thompson says as he pushes Jack into the refrigerator.

Jack finally retaliates by pushing his father solidly in the chest and knocking him off balance. He retreats across the kitchen, makes his way to the side door, and comes running outside. He catches sight of me and realizes that I saw the whole thing.

I follow Jack down the driveway.

He looks over his shoulder at me. "What do you want?" he grunts in a voice I don't even recognize.

"Get back here!" Mr. Thompson shouts.

I run after Jack to get away from the rage that lives in the house.

Chapter 7

Monday, August 7th

Summer vacation . . . is over. The first day of football practice and double sessions begins. Every player shows up for the first morning practice at 7:30 a.m.—rubbing the sleep from their eyes, trying to get used to waking up hours before their normal summer wake-up time.

The first hour of the first morning is spent with what Coach Murphy calls: "Chalk talk." He jumps right in. "Men," he explains, "the base defense we run is a 5-2. These are the different stunts out of that formation. We can blitz either the Sam or the Will linebacker. Sam is the strong side linebacker. Will is the weak side linebacker. We can also blitz the corners or the safeties out of this formation. When the linebacker goes outside and the defensive end shoots inside, we call that a twist stunt." It's now eight o'clock in the morning and Coach Murphy throws out words like Sam, Will, dart, fire, crash, twist, okie, and thunder. Our freshman coach kept things simple. Jack and I glance at each other and shake our heads. We are totally confused.

Before we start our first defensive practice, Coach Murphy says, "The depth chart explains who the starters are, who is second string, and third string. The positions listed here are not set in stone. They are based on seniority. This may change when the hitting starts on Friday and Saturday of this week."

A chill shoots through my body as everyone hoots and hollers in anticipation of our first hit day. On the way out to practice, I look on the defensive depth chart where I see that Jack and I are both second team linebackers behind the two senior starters, Ron Jacobs and Willy Canter. They're good athletes, but Jack and I know that we can win those positions. Because we worked so hard over the summer, we feel confident.

Coach Murphy blows his whistle and brings the team together. "The next four days will be about education and repetition. Put your thinking caps on and take in everything the coaches tell you."

The practice is like an assembly line: repetition, repetition, and more repetition. Coach Moses is our linebacker coach. He played at Ohio State and was an All-American. He's a monster at 6'5" and 255 pounds. His size, bald head, and goatee intimidate even the toughest players on our team.

Coach Moses starts out calmly, "This game is about hustle and hard work. As a linebacker, we work from sideline to sideline. It is imperative, absolutely necessary, that you play the ball carrier inside out." He begins to raise his voice, "NEVER, NEVER, NEVER get outside of the running back. Don't be in a hurry. The corner back's job is to turn the play back inside to you." His voice begins to get louder. "If the running back cuts back against the grain and your ass is not there, you will have a seat on the bench." Soon he is shouting. "The corner back will do his job. You do yours!" He pauses to see if we're getting it. "Is that clear?"

We all nod our heads, more out of fear than anything else.

Coach Moses, looking confident that we understand, calms down again and continues. "Your course should be down hill toward the line of scrimmage, no false reads, and no false steps. Read the offensive guards and mirror their steps. If your guard pulls, you pull with him. If he fires out at you, you meet him head on. Light him up. If he doubles on the nose guard, you fire into the gap, expect the fullback trap. Men, playing linebacker is about being a warrior. It's the most important position on the defensive side of the ball." Moses has me so fired up that I feel like I can run through a brick wall.

We practice these drills over and over until they become a part of us, ingrained in us. Moses shouts with an intensity that is contagious, "Practice does not make perfect; perfect practice makes perfect! Playing linebacker requires attitude, intensity, desire, and courage! REPETITION, REPETITION, REPETITION, until it's automatic, until you don't have to think about it."

Jack and I work together as the second group of linebackers. Coach Moses pulls Jack and me aside and says, "Keep working hard, boys."

We move on to some pass drop drills. "Men," Coach Moses says, "when you work on your pass drops make sure you open up to a forty-five degree angle and get to our drop zones." We work on pass drops for thirty minutes, breaking on passes, intercepting them, and sprinting back into line.

We end the defensive practice with a pursuit drill. One man is picked to be a rabbit who sprints all the way down the sideline, and we have to tag him before he reaches the end zone. We finish up with fifteen, forty yard sprints. If we dog it, we run extra. Everybody busts their butts, and we go into the shade for a one hour break.

Jack comes over to me and puts his hands up like he's ready to go a few rounds. He asks, "How you feeling man?"

I put my hands up in defense. "Tireless, like I'm in the best shape of my life."

Jack fakes like he's throwing out a couple jabs and dances from side to side. "Dude, I feel great, can't wait till we put the pads on and start hitting."

We sit in the shade and relax. Someone takes out a boom box, and they crank the music. Kid Rock pumps out from the speakers, "Kid Rock, I'm the real McCoy. I'm headin' out west, cause I wanna be a cowboy baby." Everyone goofs around and tells stories about their summer vacation. And before we know it, the break is over.

The second session is all offense. The first half hour is instruction. Coach Murphy is very different from Coach Moses. He slowly explains our offense. "Each player must perform his job in order for this offense to be successful. Our offense has two wide receivers, a tight end, a fullback, and a tailback." He diagrams six different plays and the blocking schemes for each play. He goes over the 34 and 35 Iso, the 38 and 39 sweep, and the 41 and 42 trap.

He finishes by saying, "The pass plays will be introduced on the third day. Running backs, be sure to hit the holes at full speed. Lineman, get to your spots with perfect technique. Offensive depth charts are on the back of the field house wall."

When the offensive instruction ends, Jack and I head to the wall to see that again we are second string behind two other seniors, John Phillips the fullback and Marc Tolliger who is the tailback. John and Marc were second string last year and got into a lot of the varsity games, especially when there was a big lead. John is big at 6'2" and 230 pounds, but he doesn't like to hit like Jack. Marc has good speed, but he doesn't have my kind of speed. Plus, I'm twenty pounds heavier. I keep reminding myself that positions will be determined on hit day.

We take the field in our gold shorts, royal blue t-shirts, and helmets. We run over the offensive plays. Coach Murphy coaches the running backs and quarterbacks. He explains the steps to the quarterbacks. Despite his knee surgery, he is super smooth. Everyone knows about his playing days at Notre Dame. He shows the steps to the tailbacks and fullbacks for each play. He says, "Make sure you have a good stance, fire out low and hard, and get to your spots at full speed. Our offense is based on timing, timing that will be perfect. Learn your play books. Learn the job of every player on every play."

Danny Towers started every game last year as a junior, and he's probably expecting a great senior year. Last year, he led Cedarville to the state semi-final game, where they lost to Mogadore. Coach Murphy treats Danny like his own son, with unlimited patience. He must see the potential for greatness.

The offensive session lasts another hour and a half. We run the same six plays over and over, trying to perfect them. Jack and I run with the second group with Jordan Walker as our quarterback Jordan started all of the junior varsity games last year, and led the team to a 10-0 record.

Jack and I anticipate each other's moves. We hustle, and our timing is perfect. I see the smile on Coach Murphy's face after each repetition that our group executes. Being the starting tailback would be a dream come true. Ever since Jack and I were little kids playing flag football, we pretended we were the starting backfield for the Cedarville Comets. We played catch in his backyard and pretended we were playing on Friday night under the lights. We created situations: the State Championship game, five seconds on the clock. I would pitch it out to him, or he would hand it off to me. We would pretend we won the State Championship for the Comets. We played until it got dark, and then we turned on the porch light until it got so dark that even the porch light wasn't enough. In 8th and 9th grade, our dream started to take shape. In 8th grade, we went undefeated, and our freshman team dominated everyone we played.

We line up for gassers at the end of practice. Gassers include running from sideline to sideline—twice. That's one repetition. We run five gassers. Backs and receivers have to run them under thirty-five seconds; linemen have to be under fifty-five. If anyone doesn't make it in time, we have to run an extra half gasser. Two kids in our group miss, so we run six gassers all together. But I don't care. I feel like I can run all day. After my first varsity practice, I am confident that Jack and I can be the starting backfield for the Cedarville Comets.

Chapter 8

August 8th to the 11th

The next two days are filled with drills, sprints, and learning new plays. Our defensive sessions are an endless repetition of linebacker drills. Coach Moses is relentless in his quest for perfection. We do pursuit drills, read your guard drills, pass drops, and shed-the-blocker techniques.

On offense we put in ten plays each day. By Wednesday, we have thirty plays: twenty running plays and ten pass plays. Jack and I pick up the offense quickly. Being in great shape makes double sessions seem easy. Because we busted our butts over the summer, we spend our time learning the offense and not worrying about having to get into shape.

At the end of practice on Wednesday, Coach Murphy reminds us, "Tomorrow is our first day of pads. Friday is our first day of contact. These hitting days will be when the starters are decided."

The fourth day of practice is an acclimation day. This is the day when we get to put on all of our pads and do some light hitting, if there is such a thing. Coaches get off saying it's a non-contact day, and then they laugh to each other, because almost all of the drills are full go. The head coach has to follow the rules, so he structures the practice so there shouldn't be a lot of hitting. However, once we got into our individual defensive groups, the drills have the taste of full contact. Coach Moses pretends not to know what the word "acclimation" means.

Jack and I are partnered up with Ron Jacobs and Willy Canter. These two guys, Jack and I never had a problem with, but on this day they become our enemies. We want to set the stage for the "hit days." Jack and I refuse to back down in the drills. We congratulate each other quietly when we get back into line. Ron and Willy had a great time over the summer partying and did not spend much time in the weight room. Their lack of conditioning is obvious during the second hour of our defensive session. Ron and Willy are constantly bent over, catching their breath. Coach Moses rides them like tired camels in the dessert.

"What the hell was that?" Moses screams. "Your steps are wrong. You're out of position. That's not the technique I showed you." He chews them out for every little mistake, knowing that their mistakes are because they are tired and out of shape. Coach Moses was in the weight room taking attendance every day. He knew the guys who were there and those who weren't.

During the offensive sessions, Jack and I work like crazy. The workouts on the track have built up our strength and our speed. We can run 100 sweeps if we have to, which is more than I can say for Marc Tolliger and John Phillips. They are better off than Ron and Willy, but they don't have the stamina that Jack and I do. We run our plays at full speed. We never shy away from contact from the scout defenses; we look forward to it, invite it.

After practice, I head to the gym where Cindy and the cheerleading squad are practicing.

When her practice is over, she walks over to where I'm sitting and says, "So, how was football?"

"Awesome. It's like pure adrenaline. I think I got a shot at starting."

"Well, why wouldn't yew? Y'all worked hard all summer. Y'all deserve it."

"It's just weird. Ever since flag football, I wanted to play varsity football, and now it's here. It's just hard to believe."

We ride our bikes home, taking in a perfect summer day. At Cindy's house, we splash each other in the pool, grab each other, and tease each other. I love touching her. I want to kiss her, but I'm almost positive I saw her mom watching out the window.

* * *

Jack and I talk on the phone, wondering who Coach Murphy will match up for the hitting drills.

"Dude, I'm so psyched," I say.

Jack responds, "We're going to pound 'em."

"Some of those seniors can barely even get through the agility drills."

"You know Murphy's going to pair us up against the starters," Jack says.

"We can beat 'em," I say confidently.

"They don't want it like we do."

The intensity in Jack's voice gets my adrenaline pumping. "You got that right. But still, I'm nervous as hell." Along with the adrenaline, the nerves start setting in.

"Yeah, me too, but we can do it. We can beat those guys. We've worked harder than they did. They might be older, but they're not better," Jack assures me.

I can feel the confidence growing. "Tomorrow, we're going to show Murphy and Moses that we deserve to be starters."

"Absolutely, we're going to kick some ass."

By now, I'm completely jacked up. I can hardly wait for tomorrow. "I'll see you tomorrow," I say to Jack.

"Get ready, bro," he says, as he hangs up the phone.

I know that Jack and I will be paired up against the first string linebackers and the first string running backs. We know, given the opportunity, we can prove to the coaches that we deserve those positions. Starting on offense and defense is our goal. I toss and turn all night in bed anticipating my first varsity hit day.

* * *

Chalk talk is brief. Coach Murphy grunts, "Our focus for today is to see who is not afraid to hit."

While we are stretching, the coaches set up cones and pads for different hitting drills like hamburger, pursuit drill, and 1-on-1 Iso drills. These are the same drills we've been doing since 8th grade.

In hamburger, both players lay on their backs. The offensive player is the ball carrier; the defensive player is the tackler. When the whistle blows, both players get to their feet as fast as they can, and there is a violent collision. I think it's just to find out who's tougher, who wants it more.

In the first drill, Jack goes up against Ron Jacobs. Jack is on D. He lies on his back, knees bent, with his fingers twitching with anticipation. There is an eerie silence, and then the whistle blows, Jack springs to his feet like a cat. Ron is slower getting up, and when he picks his head up, Jack solidly plants his face mask on his sternum. There is a loud pop of the pads. With perfect form, he lifts Ron from the ground. I swear they are five feet in the air, and Jack drives Ron backwards, slamming him into the ground. There are numerous oohs and ahhs from the players who have formed an expectant circle around the drill. Coach Moses gives Coach Murphy a look that says, I told you so.

Coach Murphy calls out, "Billy Morris and Willy Jacobs. Let's go! Let's see who wants it."

Jack and Tombo shout words of encouragement, "Come on, Billy. Light him up! Show him what you got."

Willy's friends join in. "Let's go, Willy! Let's go, baby!"

In this drill, I play the running back, and Willy is the tackler. I spring to my feet when the whistle blows. With a pure surge of adrenaline, I lower my shoulder behind a full head of steam. Willy doesn't get low enough and catches the brunt of the collision. There is a dull thud as I run over Willy and head into the end zone. Willy stays on the ground gasping for breath. The coaches go over to him. They unsnap his helmet to help him get some air. Willy finally catches his breath about a minute later and rises to one knee.

I want to go again. I know that no one can stop me. Jack and I destroy our opponents in each drill. Toward the end of the drills, Coach Murphy opens them up to anyone who feels like they have something to prove to the coaches. Jack and I look at each other and jump in. It gets to the point where no one on the team will get across from either one of us.

Finally, Jack and I face each other. Jack is the ball carrier. He lowers his shoulder, and there is an explosion when we collide. There is a loud grunt as the contact takes us over the bags that contain the drill. Our bodies fly over the bags and go crashing into the crowd of bodies that surround the drill. The players on the team want blood. It's primitive, tribal. I devour it. I eat it up. It's what I've become. And the best part about it is that my best friend is no different.

In the next drill, I carry the ball, and Jack and I lower our heads at the same time. The hit is helmet to helmet. My mind goes blank and a tiny white light zooms to the center of my brain. I stagger and fall back. I've never been hit this hard. I quickly regain my senses and jump back in the next drill. Jack and I go at it four times in a row, two best friends in a vicious battle. The popping from the pads echoes through the practice field. We both refuse to back down. The collisions are intense and violent. After a while the cheering dies down; the coaches and players stand in awe. They haven't seen this kind of intensity for a long, long time. Jack and I are sweating and bruised, but tireless. The grass between the blocking bags is torn up from the action. Today, we have made a statement. And more importantly, we have shown that no position is safe.

Coach Murphy blows his whistle. He spits his chewing tobacco on the ground as he announces to the team, "New depth charts will be posted tomorrow. You boys did a fine job today. And if you feel like you didn't have your best stuff today, there will be future opportunities to show how bad you want it." He looks over the team and taps his pen on his clipboard. "And just so you guys know, there will be some changes based on the hitting drills from today." He blows his whistle and yells, "Let's go. Line it up. We got five gassers."

Some of the guys on the team moan and groan about having to run the gassers. Jack and I jog over to the line. We can run all day.

After practice and with pounding headaches, Jack and I leave the locker room anticipating the new depth charts—with a new first string backfield and linebackers. I ride my bike over to the gym to meet Cindy. She grabs her bike, and we head toward her house.

Pedaling next to her, I start to tell her the story. "Jack and I were battling like warriors. It was awesome! You should have seen the faces on Coach Murphy and Coach Moses."

Cindy swerves from side to side. "I knew y'all could do it."

I pop a wheely on the Exploder. "We kicked some butt today. We just about killed each other."

Cindy's green eyes widen. "Look out Cedarville! Here comes Billy Morris and Jack Thompson."

Chapter 9

August 12th

The new depth charts hang from the white cinder block in the locker room. I slide my finger to the linebacker and tailback positions. I find my name and Jack's name. We did it! We earned starting positions on the varsity football team! Jack comes up behind me and pushes me on the shoulder and says, "Way to go, bro. It's me and you."

"The Billy and Jack attack!" I raise my hand for a high five.

While we dress for our sixth practice of the week, John Phillips, Marc Tolliger, Ron Jacobs, and Willy Canter mope around the locker room, and they even shoot Jack and me angry stares. They can't believe that they will be second string to two sophomores during their senior year. I don't feel bad for them. They didn't work hard over the summer, and they have to accept the consequences.

Practice includes some hitting, but mostly we focus on running plays against the scout offense and defense. We run our offensive plays over and over until the timing is perfect. It's an honor to be in the first string huddle with Danny Towers. At only seventeen years old, he is a natural leader. He commands respect in the huddle, and he runs the team like a finely tuned machine. His drops and steps are perfect. His ball fakes are smooth, like a magician. His arm is a cannon. He hits receivers on the numbers every time. He throws from a three step drop, a five step drop, a roll-out right, and a roll-out left across his body. Every one knows how hard he worked over the summer. This summer he went to three football camps: Penn State, Notre Dame, and Youngstown State because he knew they focused on the quarterback position. Even I can see that he improved over the summer, and as a senior, he will probably beat his own records from last year. Danny wants to win Cedarville a State Championship.

Practice flies by today, and I am completely jacked up about being in the first string huddle on offense. At one point, Coach Moses pulls me aside and asks, "Morris, I want you to be the leader of the defense. Do you think you can call the plays?"

"No problem. I'm your man." My heart pounds inside my chest as I think about being the leader of the defense. I do my best to take charge of the defensive huddle. I call the base defense and any stunts by the defensive line or cornerbacks. Jack gives two thumbs up to me from his position in the back of the huddle. After we break the huddle, I call the slants and adjustments from my linebacker position.

Everything seems perfect. Everything is going my way. Practice is going great. I have achieved the first part of my goal, two starting positions on the varsity football team. I prove to myself that hard work makes anything possible. Because of my dedication over the summer, my dream has become a reality. Along with Jack, I am ready to be a hometown hero.

* * *

I walk in the front door of my house and toss my football equipment into the laundry room. I can smell the pasta sauce on the stove. My mom calls to me. "Billy, come in the kitchen. There is something we need to talk about."

I enter the kitchen, and my eyes lock on Dick, who is standing directly behind my mom with his left hand on her left shoulder. He is dressed in a powder blue golf shirt and khaki pants. He also wears a devious grin.

"What do you want to talk about?" I ask.

Dick remains behind my mother and squeezes her shoulder as she talks. "Billy, honey, Richard and I have been thinking." She pauses and turns her head to look at Dick. "We've been thinking about moving, you know, out of Cedarville."

My heart stops. I try to regain my composure. "I'm not going anywhere."

"We've talked about this before. We're thinking about moving to South Carolina, somewhere warmer. Richard and I have been thinking about it for a while."

Images of leaving Cedarville flash through my mind, all the hard work and my varsity football positions, Jack, and Cindy. It's like being in a horrible dream. My whole world is a giant boulder rolling down a mountain, out of control.

"We didn't want to upset you, and we wanted to be sure it was something we wanted to do before we told you about the decision," she continues calmly.

I finally find some words. "Football just started. I found out today I'm going to be the starting varsity linebacker and tailback."

The look on my mom's face changes from certainty to uncertainty, and for a moment, she doesn't know what to say. "Listen," she gathers herself, "I know how hard you've worked this summer, but Richard and I need to get out of this town. I need to do something else with my life."

"WHAT ABOUT MY LIFE?" I shout. Then, all of what she said hits me. "Wait, what do you mean you and him?" I ask, pointing at Dick with one finger and gripping the back of the kitchen chair with my other hand.

My mom looks over her shoulder at Richard. "Well, we were thinking about sending you to Bertram. You know, where Richard went to boarding school. He says it was the best thing that ever happened to him."

"You're ripping my life away from me just so you can be in warmer weather!"

Mom fires back, "Working at that factory is all I do! I want out!"

"Why are you doing this?" I point at Dick. "It's all because of him." I narrow my eyes and clench my fists like I'm ready for a fight. Trying to steady myself and thinking of a solution, I look at my mom and say, "I can stay here and live with Jack or Cindy's family."

"No. You are not their responsibility. You are my responsibility." My mom looks at me with resolve in her eyes.

"Your responsibility that you want to ship off to boarding school, just like that!"

My mother is usually a push over, but she doesn't seem to want to budge. I think Dick has coached her. He continues to stand behind her. He's a coward, holding her out in front of him.

Feeling hopeless, I say, "There's got to be another way. Everything in my life is here. My friends, football, everything is here!"

"This is in your best interest," my mom retaliates.

"How do you know what's in *my* best interest? Cedarville is where I belong."

"Cedarville's academics are average at best. You know that. You'll get a great education at Bertram."

Dick finally speaks. "Bertram is a great school, and I'm sure you know that they won the Division IV state championship game last year. They have great teachers and a topnotch athletic program." The guy sounds like a freaking radio advertisement.

I look at him, then at my mother. I can see in my mother's eyes that her mind is made up. Their decision is final, and nothing will change it. Everything I have worked so hard for has been torn from me.

My mother, trying to comfort me, explains, "Bertram only has a nine game schedule. Their double sessions start this Monday. I already talked to the coach. You won't miss a single practice. You should pack tonight. Tomorrow we'll drive up to Cleveland and move you into your dorm."

"I am not leaving Cedarville," I yell, as I turn toward the stairs. Leaving the kitchen, I punch the wall with all my might. The plaster gives way, leaving a hole.

My mother shouts, "You get back here right now!"

I storm down the steps to the basement and slam my bedroom door, locking it behind me. I pick up the phone and call Jack. "Dude, listen to this," I start off and then give him the rundown of the bomb my mother just dropped on my life.

After a few moments of silence, Jack says, "I would ask my dad if you could come and live with us, but he can barely take care of himself, much less me and you. He's already passed out."

"I would never ask you to do that," I say. "What am I going to do? What am I going to tell Coach?"

"I don't understand why she is doing it now, without any warning?"

"I don't know. I'm sure Dick has something to do with it. That guy hasn't liked me since day one. All he ever talks about his Bertram Academy and what a star he was."

"When are you supposed to leave?" Jack asks.

"My mom says I'm supposed to pack so we can leave tomorrow. Their double sessions start on Monday. I still can't believe this."

"I wish there was something I could do."

"Yeah, me too. Listen, I'll call you tomorrow. I have to call Cindy."

"I'll stop by in the morning."

"Thanks, man."

I hang up the phone and dial Cindy's private line.

She answers in her usual cheerful voice, "Hey, Billy." There are no surprises with caller ID.

"Hey," I say, deflated and defeated.

"What's wrong?"

"Listen to this. My mom and Dick are sending me to Bertram. She said I have to pack tonight, and we're driving there tomorrow." I barely get the words out. My right hand is throbbing from punching the wall.

"Who is your mom's boyfriend to make those decisions about your life? He's not your father. Isn't there anything we can do? I can ask my dad if y'all could stay with us?"

"My mom said I'm not your family's responsibility. She said that going to Bertram is in my best interest. Period, end of discussion."

"Everything was starting to go your way."

"You're telling me."

"I am so sorry."

"Yeah, me too."

"Can I come by and see you tomorrow?"

"I was hoping you would."

"I'll be there." I can hear Cindy crying.

I hang up the phone and stare at the ceiling. I think about how this change will affect my life. I think about Cindy, and Jack, and playing for Cedarville with my best friends. It will be more than just moving. It will be leaving friends that are more like brothers. I punch my heavy bag in my room with my already sore hand until my knuckles start to bleed and the tears run down my cheeks. I wipe the tears from my face, and reach down into the angriest part of my soul and promise myself to never cry again.

Chapter 10

August 13th

On Sunday morning, Jack comes to my house early. He sits across from me in his sleeveless Cedarville football shirt. Just looking at the shirt makes me miss being here already.

"I'll keep you posted on everything that's going on," he says trying to make me feel better.

In Jack's face, I can see his sincerity and appreciate his friendship more than ever. He adjusts his baseball hat over his curly brown hair.

"You got time for a quick game of PlayStation?" Jack asks.

"Why not?" I say as I load the college football game.

For forty-five minutes Jack and I talk about flag football games, tree houses, and all the good times we had growing up in Cedarville. We talk about our first day as freshmen, dances, detentions, and summer nights at the drive-in with Cindy and Leigh.

Before he leaves, Jack takes his silver chain off his neck. It has a silver medal on it. On one side is St. Michael. The other side is St. Christopher standing on a mountaintop fighting off dragons. He hands it to me. "Here," he says. "Whenever I get upset, I just hold on to St. Christopher. See, he's killing all those dragons."

I shake my head. "I can't take this from you. It's from your mom."

Jack puts the medal in my hand. "Just don't lose it, okay?"

I reluctantly take the chain from Jack because I can see that he's sincere, that he wants me to have it. I fasten it around my neck. "I won't lose it. Thanks."

A knock comes at my bedroom door. Jack says, "Take care of yourself."

We give each other a high five and lean in for a half hug. He says hello to Cindy as he walks upstairs. I hear him say goodbye to my mom as he walks out the front door.

Cindy tries to hide her face. Her bright green eyes are bloodshot. "This was supposed to be our year."

I don't even know what to say. "This wasn't my decision."

With a hopeful look, Cindy says, "My parents actually said y'all could stay with us."

I shrug my shoulders. "My mom already said no way to that idea."

Cindy holds my hand. "I don't want you to go."

"I don't want to go either." When I look at Cindy, I begin to realize how much I care about her.

My mom calls from upstairs. "Billy c'mon, we've got to get going."

I give Cindy a hug. She takes my face in both of her hands and brings my lips to hers, and she kisses me. I didn't know how much emotion could be conveyed with a kiss, but Cindy manages to show me how much she cares about me with that one kiss. I don't want to let go.

At the front door, she looks at me and says, "Call me."

"You got it." I walk her to the end of my driveway.

She pulls out a CD. "Here," she says. "I made this for yew last night."

Looking down I say, "I didn't make you one."

Cindy waves it off. "Y'all got enough to deal with."

"Thanks."

"Just don't forget to call." She wipes the tears from her eyes and gives me a huge hug.

When I walk back into the house, I head down the basement and call Coach Murphy. He picks up. "Coach, it's Billy, Billy Morris."

"What's up, Morris? You okay? You stub your toe or something?"

"Not quite. I've uh, got some bad news." This is harder than I thought. "My mom's decided to move to South Carolina, and she's sending me to Bertram Academy."

Coach Murphy is silent on the other end of the line. After what seems like forever, he speaks up. "I hope you understand that your mother is doing what she feels is best for you. Sometimes, decisions like this are beyond our control. I'm real sorry to hear that. We're going to miss you, son. But, I want you to know something. I want you to know that I am real proud of how you worked this summer. You are one of the hardest workers on this team. Just remember wherever you go and whatever you do, you will be successful because of the kind of person you are. You just keep working hard. Whatever you do, don't ever give up. We're sorry to see you go."

Coach Murphy's words make me feel proud, and at the same time, I feel like I'm letting down the entire town. "Sorry for letting you down."

"Billy, this isn't your fault. Make the best of the situations that life throws at you. I have some news for you. Life isn't always good and easy. There are going to be lots of obstacles. You have to face that stuff head on."

I feel a regret that I will not play for Coach Murphy, or Coach Moses. "Coach, thanks for everything. I'll make you proud at Bertram."

"Good luck, son."

I say goodbye and hang up the phone.

My mom calls from downstairs, "Billy, let's go. Put your stuff in the car. We need to get going." Unfortunately, when I make it upstairs, I see that Dick is going to Cleveland with us. I completely ignore Dick, and my mother gives me an angry look. I pack two large suitcases and a backpack into the trunk of our silver Buick.

We drive north. After five freeways and four hours of complete silence, we pull up to the entrance of the school where the large, cast iron gates greet us. We pass open fields, tennis courts, and large brick buildings. The long winding driveway is lined with giant maple and oak trees in full bloom. It eventually leads to the red brick admissions office covered in ivy.

Dick breaks the silence. "Ah, yes, the old stomping grounds. Got some great memories from my time here at Bertram. I remember my senior year, had twenty-two tackles in one game. Got my name on a plaque on the wall of fame." I am silent, still feeling betrayed.

Coach Murphy's words echo in my mind. *Make the best of the situation. Life is full of unexpected obstacles. You need to face them head on.*

My mother interrupts my thoughts. "Look, there are some of the football players. They must be here for double sessions." As she utters these words, we turn the corner. There is a sign posted on the gate that reads: *Football Check-in and Student Registration.* My mother parks the car in a lot that is half full. I expect to see Mercedes and Porsches, but I am surprised to see both nice cars and a few beaters.

In the gym, forty or so guys are registering for their rooms and receiving their itineraries for practice. I stand in line next to a boy whose face I recognize. He has blond hair and blue eyes and a flattop haircut. He has on a gray t-shirt with cut off sleeves that expose his well-defined biceps. I remember playing against him as a freshman at Cedarville. The kid recognizes me and says, "Hey, aren't you Billy Morris?"

"Yeah, that's me."

He reaches out his hand. "I'm Sean, Sean Foran. I played against you last year. I played for Tipp City."

"I remember you. You're one of the toughest hitters we faced all year." Sean's face lights up with the compliment.

"You guys were the best team we played all year. We couldn't stop you and your fullback. What's his name?"

"Jack Thompson," I answer, feeling proud but sad to hear his name.

"Yeah, Thompson, that's it." Sean shakes his head and smiles. "Man, that dude was tough."

Sean and I start talking like old friends. Last year we were bitter rivals, but our common situation brings us together almost immediately. Sean and I get our room assignments. I am in room 42 on the fourth floor. Sean's room assignment is the same; we are roommates. Sean seems to be as happy as I am. At least we won't be rooming with total strangers. We look over our itineraries. There is a meeting tonight with the football team, and then I start double sessions all over again. Tomorrow, I will have to go about proving myself to a whole new set of coaches and a whole new team.

Looking around the room, I notice that a lot of the athletes at Bertram are good-sized kids. Most are returning after a year when they won the Division IV state championship. I followed their season in articles from the newspaper. They have a bunch of players returning for their senior year. It won't be easy to earn a spot on this team. I know that the tailback position is already filled by Terrance Strong, a returning starter from the year before. He was named All-Ohio. I figure he will be one of the people I will be competing with for the position of tailback. I'm not sure who the linebackers are, but I am sure that my work will be cut out for me. I do have one advantage. I already went through the soreness of my first week of double sessions, and I feel strong.

Sean and I check into our room. Dick and my mother help me carry my things to my room, which is on the fourth floor. There is no elevator. For once in my life, I am glad that Dick is with us. My mother unpacks my things and helps to get my room situated. She asks, "So, what do you think?"

"Does it matter?" I look around my new room. There are two desks, two closets and two bunk beds.

"I think this is a great place, a great opportunity." My mom places my backpack on the floor, and Dick puts one of my suitcases on the bed.

"If you say so," I say in a sarcastic tone.

"You're going to be fine." My mom opens my suitcase and starts to take out some of the clothes. She puts some t-shirts in the top drawer of the dresser.

"Whatever you say."

She grabs some dress shirts and hangs them in the closet. She pulls out some sheets and starts to put them on the bed. As she slides my pillow into a pillowcase, she says, "I really think this is going to be a good thing for you."

"Mom, I think this," I open my arms like I'm showing her my new room, "is something that's going to be good for *you*, not me."

She takes a deep breath, probably considering whether or not now is a good time to get into it. She says, "We have a long ride back to Cedarville, so we'll let you settle in." She gives me a hug. "I love you."

I feel a surge of panic, and my heart starts to pound. I have never lived on my own before. I start to say something, but I stop myself. I promised myself I wouldn't show any emotion, so I don't.

I see in my mother's face a sense of uncertainty; I can tell that she is having second thoughts about her decision.

She hugs me again and says, "Study hard, keep up the good work on the football field, eat well, and call me. I'll miss you."

I don't even bother to say goodbye to Dick, who I'm sure, is already celebrating the fact that he doesn't have to deal with me anymore.

I begin to unpack the rest of my things. From my fourth story window, I see my mom and Dick walking across the parking lot and climbing into the silver Buick. I watch as the car snakes down the winding road from the academy.

Sean comes walking in the room, slaps me on the back and says, "Team meeting is in thirty minutes. Better start getting ready."

Sean unpacks his things as he tells me his story, which is much different from mine. "Man, I am just glad to be here. This is an opportunity of a lifetime. Things in Tipp City weren't looking too good. You know, we don't have a lot of good athletes."

When we played against Sean, our team dominated the game. Sean was the only kid that could actually play. Their varsity team wasn't much better. They hadn't won more than five games in a season over the last five years.

Sean says, "I want to play for a winner. My dad pulled some strings to get me into Bertram."

I tell Sean my story about how my mom and Dick turned my life inside out.

"You gave up two varsity positions as a sophomore?" Sean says, with a look of complete shock. "Man, that is a raw deal."

"Yeah, well. I guess I gotta make the best of it." I sit down on my bed.

Sean continues to unpack his things. "It's weird. I'm excited to be here, and you wish you didn't have to be."

"I guess it's all how you see it."

"Yeah, I guess so." He throws some jeans into an empty drawer.

"So, I guess that meeting starts in about ten minutes?"

Sean finishes unpacking the rest of his clothes and says, "Yeah, we better get going."

* * *

At the field house, we have our first meeting with the coaches of Bertram Academy. The field house has metal chairs lined up in front of a stage with a podium. The coach walks past the podium, down from the stage and stands in front of his team. The coach is not a big man, maybe only 5'7", but I can tell that he commands respect. He doesn't laugh or joke around. His salt and pepper hair is neatly combed, and his red and gray collared coaching shirt is tucked into his black coaching shorts. When he gets to the front of the team, there is complete silence.

"Welcome everybody. I am Coach Carlson. These are my assistants: Linebacker Coach and Defensive Coordinator Coach Kaplan, Defensive Back and Wide Receiver Coach, Coach Stevens, Offensive and Defensive Line Coach, Coach Benjamin. I will be coaching the running backs and quarterbacks as well as calling the plays. Coach Kaplan will be calling the defense. As I look around, I see some old faces and some new faces. We had an unbelievable season last year winning the Division IV State Championship. With the returning starters from last year, I believe that we should be able to repeat that accomplishment this year. Hopefully, all of you put in the necessary work this summer to achieve that goal." He looks around at all the players and gives a little smile. "Well, we'll figure that out soon enough once practice starts tomorrow. I am proud to say that we have some new players joining us this year. My advice to you new players is don't sit back. Don't let other people take charge. Even though we have a lot of returning starters, that doesn't mean the positions will be handed to them this year. All positions will be earned. Also, for all new players, I will go over the dorm rules." A groan comes from all of the players. "There is a nine o'clock curfew, and lights are out at ten. Don't try me on these rules. If you are out past curfew, you will be written up. Three write ups, and you will be on probation, which means no football. Is that clear?" His jaws work hard on the piece of gum in his mouth.

"Yes, Coach," the team replies in unison.

"And finally," Coach Carlson adds while chomping on his gum, "our first double session starts tomorrow at 8 a.m. Don't be late. If you can't be on time, be on Coach Carlson time, and that's ten minutes early. I expect great things from this team. Tonight, look over and learn the first ten pages of the offensive playbook and the first ten pages of your defensive playbook. Pay particular attention to your position and what you are supposed to do on each play. Also, pay attention to what all the other positions are doing so you can understand the scheme of our offense and defense. Come prepared tomorrow. The first three days will be without pads, the fourth day will be with pads, and on the fifth day, we start hitting."

With that announcement, all the players, except for me, whoop and yell at the anticipation of the first day of hitting. Coach Carlson finishes, "Men, seniors especially, this is your team; make this year special."

That night, Sean and I go over our playbooks together. Bertram runs a similar offense and defense to Cedarville. Sean struggles a little bit. I explain the new formations to him, and he starts to pick things up.

When we finish, Sean turns out the light and gets into his bed on the opposite side of the room. I walk over to the fourth story window, slide it open, and look outside. A cool breeze floats in the window. I scan the lit-up campus and look up at the stars that illuminate the night sky. The moon is full. I open up the case that holds the mix CD from Cindy and put it in my brown Pioneer boom box. I turn the volume down so I don't bother Sean. The first song is Staind's *Outside*. It's the live version where he performs with Fred Durst from Limp Bizkit. As the guitar strums out the chords, I consider the events that took place in the last twenty-four hours and have a hard time believing that this is my reality. I look down on the old brick buildings and the large campus that make up my new home. The song pours from the speakers and the lyrics say, "Tomorrow will be okay."

Chapter 11

August 14th

I wake up to unfamiliar surroundings and a cold morning breeze from our still-open window from the night before. Sean is snoring in the bed on the other side of the dorm room. My nightmare from yesterday has become my reality. I am really here, at Bertram Academy. I want someone to pinch me and wake me up, tell me it's all a dream. As I stare at the few cracks on the ceiling, I think about Jack and the guys from Cedarville and how they will be practicing today, and how their lives will go on. My positions will be filled. My name will be erased from the depth chart in the coach's office, just like that, with one swipe of the eraser, and Billy Morris is gone—out of sight, out of mind. In the middle of thinking about Cedarville, it occurs to me that I forgot to call Cindy last night. I go to grab my phone before I realize she is probably on her way to cheerleading practice.

Sean stirs in his bed and rolls over. In a groggy, early-morning voice he says, "Hey, man, what's up?"

"I just can't believe this. I already did my first week of double sessions."

Sean sits up, resting on his elbows. "Just think, you're one step ahead of the game. You're already in good shape. This week will be easy for you."

"I guess we'll find out," I mumble.

Sean is a fullback and linebacker, so we will be in competition with each other for the starting linebacker position. It's one of the only positions on defense that they need to fill. Almost the entire defense is returning from last year. It is rare for a group of juniors to win a state championship.

The field house is walking distance from the football field. Sean and I jog down the gravel road past the freshly cut field hockey and lacrosse fields on our left. Off in the distance are two baseball diamonds on the left and two soccer fields on the right. At the end of the gravel road is the football stadium with red-painted bleachers. A huge eagle sculpture sits at the entrance to the stadium. The sign reads: Bertram Eagles: Division IV State Champions: 2002. I get the chills as I walk past the eagle. At the field house, we pull out our play books, and Coach Carlson addresses the team. "Men," he begins, "these will be the running plays we will put in today. I cannot stress enough the importance of timing and teamwork. Each person needs to know everyone's job." I wonder if all head coaches give the same speech on the first day of double sessions.

Out on the field, we begin running through our offensive groups. I'm in the tailback group with Terrance Strong. He's a stud, not that big, maybe five-eleven, but he can fly. He glides on the field, almost effortlessly. The football field is his natural habitat, like he was born there.

During a break, I ask Sean, "How did Terrance end up at Bertram?"

"Two years ago, he transferred from East Cleveland, played wide receiver as a sophomore, but last year he was the starting tailback, got an athletic scholarship. He's got like 4.5 speed. It looks like he got even faster over the summer. Did you see him run those plays? Man, he's fast."

"Yeah, you can say that again. The guy is like a freak of nature." The sun beats down and the humidity rises as we start our offensive session in the afternoon. I run with the third group of backs, which isn't very impressive because there are only three groups. Bertram does not have many players;

there are only thirty-two all together. My new job is to get water from the trainer for the starting offense and defense. In a matter of two days, I've gone from first-string-varsity to third-string-water-boy, but I refuse to feel sorry for myself.

I run each drill at full speed. The week with Cedarville makes practice at Bertram seem easy. Even though our third string quarterback is just learning the plays, I help him and Sean out. Sean plays fullback with my group. The only advantage of being in the third group is that we have the opportunity to see the play run twice before we actually have to do it. We work well together. Sean has good speed and always manages to get out of the way of pitches on sweeps, and he hits the holes hard.

In between plays I say to Sean, "I think we can move up to second string when the hitting drills start. The two juniors are not that strong. The only thing they got on us is that they ran the same offense last year. Terrance and Sammy, on the other hand, those guys look like they should be in the freaking NFL."

Terrance Strong stands deep in the I formation and explodes from his stance, faster than anybody I have ever seen. The fullback, Sammy Jones, is just as awesome. Sammy and Terrance move like one person, anticipating each other's moves.

There's a better chance to start on defense. There are only four linebackers, and Sean and I are two of them. One of them is a junior, who looks to be a decent athlete. The other linebacker is Marcus Tyler. At 5' 8" and 225 pounds, he is called the "bowling ball."

The linebacker coach, Coach Kaplan, puts Marcus and the junior, Joey Tate, as the starters. I run in the second group with Sean. Coach Kaplan says, "For those of you who don't know, I played for the University of Michigan. I was an All-American. If you boys dedicate yourselves and work hard, one day, you can be an All-American. The groups you've been placed in are for learning the base defense. Pay attention and learn your reads."

I run the drills with the knowledge I received from Coach Moses. After watching the other players go through the drills, I know that I have a shot at starting at linebacker.

After our individual defensive drills, Coach Kaplan pulls me aside. "Mr. Morris," he says, "who taught you to play linebacker?"

"My coach at Cedarville," I utter proudly. "He played middle linebacker at Ohio State."

"Ohio State, huh." He shakes his head and smiles. "Well, even though you learned your skills from a Buckeye, your steps are good, your pursuit is downhill, and you make no false steps. You do a nice job reading the guards, and your pass drops are solid." He slaps me on the helmet. "If you can hit, we might just have a spot for you on the varsity."

I smile proudly as I walk away. The first day of doubles at Bertram is easy compared to Cedarville. On the way back to the dorm, Cindy and Jack are on my mind. I wonder how Cindy is doing with cheerleading. I want to talk to Jack to see who Coach Murphy replaced me with. Marc Tolliger will probably get to start at tailback, even though he didn't do anything over the summer. Willy Canter will probably be the starting linebacker with Jack.

Suddenly, my stomach starts to turn. I realize that I have been so caught up in the moving out of my house, moving into my new dorm, and trying to earn a spot on my new team, that I forgot about what I left behind. I think about playing under the lights in Cedarville with the entire town watching. I can almost hear the loudspeaker shouting out my name and then Jack's name: *Starting at Fullback for the Cedarville Comets, sophomore Jack Thompson, and starting at Tailback for the Cedarville Comets, sophomore Billy Morris.* I picture the scene in my head. The blue and gold colors scattered throughout the stands. Cindy is cheering with her face painted with a flying Comet on each cheek with little yellow stars around it. I can hear the band playing and drums pounding as we sprint out onto the field—a dream come true.

When I get back to my dorm, I grab my cell phone and walk out onto the campus and call Cindy. The phone rings four or five times until she answers.

"Hello."

"Hey."

"Billy, is that yew?"

"Yeah, it's me."

"Why haven't y'all called? Are y'all okay? How are y'all doing?"

I try to answer the flurry of questions one at a time. "Well, let's see. I've been driving with my mother and Dick, checking into my dorm, trying to make it through doubles at a new school where I barely know anyone. And to top it off, I miss you, Jack, and everyone else. I haven't had a minute to call, and when I finally thought about it, it was too late."

Cindy backs off. "I've been worried. I haven't stopped thinking about y'all. I feel like it's all been some horrible dream."

"I know. It's been crazy. We still have two weeks of practice before school starts." I think about Cedarville finishing up practice.

"So, what's the school like?" Cindy asks.

"It's all right I guess. It's a prep school, but the only thing I'm prepared to do is get out of here."

"Y'all are going to be fine," Cindy says, trying to reassure me. "If anybody can do this, it's yew. Those guys are lucky to have yew."

"Thanks. That means a lot." Even though Cindy's voice makes me feel better, it makes me miss her even more.

"Are y'all doing okay?" she asks.

"I guess I'm doing fine, but we do have a curfew."

"A curfew? Seriously, what time?"

"Lights out at ten."

"That's early."

"I know. I want to talk some more, but I should go. I want to call Jack before lights out. I told him I would."

"I understand. I'll talk to y'all tomorrow."

I say goodbye and call Jack. I know it's late, and I don't want to wake up his dad. Luckily, Jack picks up after the first ring.

"Hello?"

"Jack?"

"Billy, I was hoping you'd call. What's up, bro?" Jack asks.

"Just trying to get through this nightmare."

"Nightmare, huh? How's football going?"

"Dude, doubles are easy here compared to Cedarville. The coach here runs things more low key."

"You got a chance to start?" Jack asks.

"The tailback position looks pretty locked up. You remember Terrance Strong. That guy is just plain fast. I don't think I have a shot there, but I think there's a spot on the defense at linebacker. If I get it, I'll be the only sophomore starter."

"Good for you man, do it. We all miss you. I talked to Cindy after practice yesterday. She's super bummed about you leaving. I told her you guys would keep in touch, and that everything would be okay."

"Thanks man. I appreciate it. I've been worried about her. I've been worried about me."

"You'll be fine; just keep at it."

"I wish I felt that way. I'm still so pissed at my mom and Dick."

"There is a For Sale sign on your front yard, looks like they're serious about leaving."

"I try not to think about it." To change the subject I ask, "By the way, how's the football team doing?"

"It's good. Coach Moses named me the defensive captain. I couldn't believe it. After you left, I started running the defensive huddle and calling all the plays. He said I was born to be a linebacker. I got all jacked up, wanted to lay somebody out. I can't wait for our first scrimmage this weekend, only two more weeks until our first game."

"That's cool," is all I can get out. Hearing about all the good things happening to Jack in Cedarville makes me jealous. He's the captain of the defense; that was my job. "Listen man, I have to run. Lights go out at ten. Good job being named captain."

Jack must recognize something in my voice. After a long silence, Jack says, "Billy, you're like a brother to me. You're going to be okay. Show those prep school boys how we do it at Cedarville. You'll be the starting linebacker, kicking some ass. You know those guys don't have what you got. You worked too hard this summer to let them take what's yours."

"You know, you're right." I can feel my spirit lifting.

"Let me know how the hitting goes. I want to know if those private school boys have any courage."

"You got it, man! I'm going to show 'em what Cedarville football is all about. You're a real friend."

"You better light somebody up for me."

"You got it, bro. I'll call you later."

"Later."

Chapter 12

August 18th to 23rd

Over the next three days, we put in play after play on offense and overload our playbooks with defensive schemes. Coach Carlson stresses the strategic part of the game more than Coach Murphy. Coach Carlson has great players, but not much depth. He puts the right players in the right positions. He moves players around, giving them new positions as the weeks go by. There is not one selfish player on the team. When players are asked to move to a new position, they just do it—without question. I guess they figure it's in the best interest of the team, and usually in a short period of time, that player excels at his new position. Coach Carlson understands personnel in the game of football. With a limited number of players, he created a small-school powerhouse. Of course, it doesn't hurt when All-State tailback Terrance Strong is in your backfield.

* * *

It's on our fourth day of practice, the acclimation day, that Terrance and I have our first run in. Because I'm a second string linebacker, I play on the scout defense. We hold these huge blocking bags, while the first offense blasts into them to perfect their blocking scheme.

Coach Carlson calls the plays on the offensive side of the ball. The offense is smooth. Ten of the eleven players, except for the quarterback, Mike Giffin, are seniors and returning starters from the State Championship team. Their flawless execution shows why they won State. Because Terrance and I have not yet been introduced, I am just the new sophomore, a nobody. On a dive play he runs through the line of scrimmage. My offensive lineman misses his block, and I am one on one with Terrance. The only problem is that I have a huge blocking bag. He makes a quick move and jukes to the outside. I lunge to hit him with the bag and miss. He laughs at me while running toward the end zone. On the way back to the huddle, he throws the ball, and it hits me in the back of the helmet.

Terrance has pissed off the wrong guy.

I ask Coach Kaplan, who runs the scout defense, "Can I get rid of this stupid bag?"

He shakes his head. "Don't worry about it. Practice is for the offensive team. They need to get a good look."

Jack's words ring in my ears. *Show those prep school boys how we do it.*

Before the next play, I decide not to use the blocking bag. I line up over the guard in our 52 defense. The guard pulls, and I read sweep. I drop the bag, and I take my course toward the running back. Making no false steps, my course is downhill toward the line of scrimmage. My technique is perfect. Avoiding the blocking from the inside, I maneuver behind the pulling guard. Playing inside out like I was taught at Cedarville, I shoot through the gap and meet Terrance head on in the hole and place my facemask on the ball and execute a perfect form tackle. There is a loud pop. I wrap his legs with my arms and pull them to my chest. Terrance grunts as I lift him off his feet during the violent collision and drive him into the ground. I step on his hand and push off on his facemask to stand up. I glare down at him and tell him, "Stay Down."

In an instant, Terrance is on his feet up in my face. Coaches and teammates come running and try to get between us. The offense is pushing and shoving, and to my surprise, the scout defense has my back, led by Sean Foran. Bodies are flying everywhere.

Terrance is in the thick of the mob shouting every swear word he knows and shouts, "I"M GONNA KILL YOU, NEXT CHANCE I GET."

I point my finger at Terrance and tell him, "YOU'RE NOT GOOD ENOUGH TO BE RUNNING YOUR MOUTH."

"I'M GONNA TEAR YOU APART," Terrance threatens.

"I'M RIGHT HERE. NOT AFRAID OF YOU," I shout back.

The pushing and shoving continues for what seems like an eternity. Coach Carlson finally blows his whistle as loud as he can four or five times in a row until the two groups quiet down and are separated by the coaches. Each group is standing shoulder to shoulder unwilling to give any ground. The scout defense made a stand. Maybe we are just sophomores, but we are football players. We deserve to be treated like members of the team. I'm sure Coach Carlson isn't too thrilled that I just stuck his All-State tailback, but I hope he feels like he found someone who is fearless and loves to play the game the way it should be played. There is still one more spot on the starting defense at linebacker, and nobody wants it more than me.

After we hit the showers, I make my way back to my dorm on campus. Out of the corner of my eye I see Terrance coming right at me. I stand my ground, expecting a right hook. Instead, he walks up to me and extends his hand. I give him a funny look, and he shakes his head and says, "Friends?"

"You and me?" I ask.

"We're a team. Coach sat me down, said I had it coming. Said you put me in my place, and that might've been a good thing."

"No worries." I reach out my hand to shake his.

"We cool, Morris?"

"Yeah, we're cool."

So that was that. A little controversy earned me some respect, a lesson that I would not forget. *No matter what, stand up for yourself.*

* * *

The next day is full go, hit day. I am up before the alarm goes off. I stare at the wall and my Ray Lewis poster. Just looking at the poster gets me fired up.

Sean wakes up with the alarm. He rubs his eyes and sits up in his bed. He looks at me and sees that I've been up. "What's up man?" he asks.

"Can't sleep. Not on days like this."

Sean puts his feet on the cool white tiled floor and says groggily, "Hey man, time to earn a position. You think coach will put you against Terrance after yesterday."

"I doubt it. The farther away I am from Terrance the better."

Sean and I will be in competition for the starting linebacker spot. When hit day comes around, I put myself in a different world. I go into the zone, a place where things are nasty and intense. I have no friends on hit day. It isn't about friendship; it's about football, survival, and courage. If you don't approach it that way, then you usually spend most of your time on the bench as a spectator. I am not a good spectator.

It is my second hit day with my second team in only two weeks. I am proud of the way I am handling being the new kid at the new school. It isn't easy.

* * *

Coach Carlson starts practice. "Men, today is the day you've been waiting for. Today is a chance to earn a position. We have each player partnered up. After that, you can jump in as many drills as you can."

We head out for stretching and warm-up laps. After warm-up laps, we are put into our hitting groups. I am partnered up with Joey Tate. Joey is a good athlete, but hitting is not his strong point. On the first drill, I run him over, making him wish he was a wide receiver. He walks out of the drill with his head down.

In the next drill, I am up against Sean. I remember from last year that he is a tough kid, but no match for me today. The drills with Sean are intense. In one, Sean is the ball carrier, and I am the defender. It is a pursuit drill that brings us into a head-on collision. I take a good course and lower my shoulder. I wrap up Sean and drive him four yards out of bounds.

Sean jumps to his feet and slaps me on the helmet and says, "Nice hit." Sean's too nice.

In between sessions, Coach Kaplan pulls me aside. "Billy, you think you're ready to start on the varsity?"

I look Coach Kaplan in the eye, "It's all I want."

He pats me on the back and says, "Good, you'll be starting at linebacker with Marcus."

I nod my head and feel energized. I can't wait to tell Jack.

After practice Sean says, "Coach Kaplan told me he I did a good job today. He said I'd be second-string linebacker and share time at nose guard. What did he tell you?"

"I'll be starting linebacker with Marcus—not to let him down."

Sean slaps me on the shoulder pads. "Congratulations, man. Way to go."

Sean is not only a good athlete, but he's becoming a good friend. At the afternoon practice, I take my spot in the defensive huddle as the weak side linebacker, the scrape-backer. Marcus is the fill-backer. His job is to fill the holes; my job is to scrape along the defensive line and punish the ball carrier. I'm glad that I was at Cedarville for the first week of practice. Coach Moses taught me more than technique. He taught me about attitude, that believing you can do something is sometimes just as important as doing it. I learned to believe in myself, to stand up for myself, and gained the confidence to earn the starting linebacker position at Bertram.

After practice on Saturday, I realize that summer weekends are dead at Bertram. I try calling Cindy, but her dad tells me she is out, that she went to the drive-in with some friends. I call over at Jack's house, and his father answers the phone. I can't understand him with his slurred speech. He hangs up the phone, and I never figure out where Jack is. On my bed, even though I am only three and half hours from Cedarville, I feel like I'm a million miles away.

Sean lumbers into the room, checks his spiky blond hair in the mirror and says, "Hey man. What's up?"

"Not much, trying to get a hold of some of my friends back home."

"Feeling homesick?" Sean asks.

Looking down, I say, "Yeah, I guess you could say that. I grew up with those guys. They're like family. You know, brothers."

Sean nods. "Yeah, I totally understand. I had a bunch of good friends back home, but there was no future there. Tipp City football is horrible, and school was a joke. I never did any homework. I want to go to a good college. I couldn't have done that in Tipp."

"School has never been at the top of my list."

"Well, you better put school at the top of your list. From what I hear, Bertram is pretty tough."

Sean and I end up sitting up until two in the morning talking about school, friends, and sports. Turns out, we have a ton of things in common. Sean tells me about his girlfriend. He gets a bunch of letters from her. She always signs them, Love Denise, and she sprays her perfume on them. Because he doesn't have a cell phone, I tell him he can use mine whenever he wants to.

Chapter 13

August 24th

It's Sunday morning, and we have the day off—no practice. I am up early, and Sean is still sleeping. I don't want to bother him, so I quietly get up, get dressed, and I walk toward the cafeteria for breakfast. As I stroll through the center of campus, I notice a sign posted on the gymnasium door that reads: Field Hockey Registration.

Finally, I think, girls. The one good thing about Bertram is that it is co-ed. Some of the private schools around here are either all-boys or all-girls. Thank God I won't be surrounded by a bunch of guys all the time.

On the way to the cafeteria, I can smell the bacon and eggs outside the door. After filling my plate, I sit in the corner of the dining hall looking through the giant picture window with a view of the campus. I sit and eat in silence, taking in the trees and what seems like miles of green grass. I'm the only one there, except for the ladies serving breakfast.

Walking through campus, I lock eyes with this girl. She has brown hair and a dark complexion. She has a bag in one hand, and a field hockey stick in the other. I can't stop staring at her. I'm amazed when she walks right up to me and asks, "Hey, do you know where the field hockey registration is?"

"They are . . . uh, um . . . in the . . . uh . . . gym."

79

She shows her perfect teeth. "I know it's in the gym, but where's the gym?"

"Oh," I laugh to myself. "I can take you there. It's just around the corner." I put my hand out and say, "By the way, my name is Billy, Billy Morris."

"Nice to meet you, Billy." She puts her stick in her other hand that holds the bag, and she shakes my hand. "I'm Erin." She looks me up and down, "So, what are you doing here so early before school starts?"

"Football. We started last week. It's been pretty quiet around here. It's good to see some new faces. What about you?"

"Transferred from my old school down in Columbus—Granville High—near Denison."

"I've heard of Denison. Some guys I know went there to play ball." I feel like a meathead. Is football the only thing I can talk about? "So this is your first year here, like me?"

"Yeah, but I think I already said that," Erin says.

"Right, you did." I want to punch myself in the head.

Erin pushes my shoulder. "I'm just teasing you."

I don't know what comes over me because I'm shy as hell around girls, but I find some courage. "Hey," I stumble, "maybe we could get something to eat later or something?"

"You asking me out?" Erin tilts her head to the side.

I hold my hands up like I'm stopping traffic. "Um, just as friends. You know, two new students."

Erin looks down for a moment. "Yeah that sounds nice. Where's your dorm?"

"I'm staying at Stuart Hall. It's on the south side of campus. How about I meet you here at the gym at six tomorrow after practice? Dinner's at 6:30."

"It's a deal."

We arrive at the gym, and I point Erin in the direction of the registration. She thanks me and goes inside.

On the way back to the dorm, I can't stop thinking about Erin. I think about that first moment when I saw her. I think about how she moves. How she smiles with her perfect teeth and perfect lips. How she smells, dizzying. I think about her tanned legs, strong and athletic. I can't stop thinking about how beautiful she is, did I just say beautiful? I never talk like that. I usually use words like cute, hot, or smokin'. I've never seen anyone like her.

And then, out of nowhere, the thought of Cindy pops into my mind. Sean and I talked so late that I forgot to call her. She's going to be pissed. I take my phone out of my bag and dial Cindy's number.

We talk about school, football, and cheerleading. But during the entire conversation with Cindy, I can't stop thinking about Erin.

* * *

Monday begins our second week of double sessions. We are preparing for a scrimmage at the end of the week. Our first game is on Saturday after the first week of school. Bertram plays all home games on Saturday afternoon, a tradition that will take some getting used to. As a freshman at Cedarville, I dreamed about playing under the lights on Friday night. At least our away games will be played on Friday nights, but I'm disappointed that our home games won't.

Practice is tough in the humid Ohio heat. The thermometer on the side of the field house reads that it's ninety degrees today, and the humidity is unbearable. It's the kind of heat that stops you in your tracks; it feels like you can swim through it. I run in the second group on offense and start to feel more comfortable with my starting position at linebacker. I learn all of the stunts and the defensive calls. The senior leadership keeps everyone in line. Even though I'm missing my friends from Cedarville, I can't help but think that Bertram Academy has a chance to be state champions again this year.

After practice, I head back to the dorm at 3:30. After I wake up from a solid nap, I jump out of bed and run to the shower to get ready for my dinner with Erin. I don't want to smell. After I shave off my stubble, I splash on some Axe cologne and dash out the door. It's 6:25.

I see Erin standing under the willow tree in the center of campus, and suddenly everything starts to move in slow motion. The wind picks up and blows across the campus. Her hair flies back, just like in the movies. She looks awesome, better than I remember from yesterday. I have to catch my breath.

"Hey," she jumps toward me.

"What's up?"

"Not much. We just finished practice. I'm exhausted. Come on, let's eat."

While we walk toward the cafeteria, there is an awkward silence. We open the doors, and join the food line. Everything smells really good. We make small talk as we move through the line to get our food. I load my plate with mashed potatoes and roast beef, and Erin makes a salad. We find a table in the back of the cafeteria.

Erin asks, "How was practice today?"

"Things are okay. This is actually my third week of practice. I already have a week under my belt from my old school."

"Where did you go to school before?"

"Cedarville, it's just south of Dayton." I take a big bite of mashed potatoes.

"So what brings you to Bertram?" she asks.

I scratch my head, knowing the story is hard to explain. "Well, you see, my mom and her boyfriend decided to move. They weren't sure what to do with me. So here I am."

"Makes you feel kind of unimportant." Erin takes a sip from her Diet Coke.

"Yeah, it pretty much sucks. I earned two spots on the varsity team with my best friend Jack. This was going to be our year." I catch myself. I'm rambling, and I'm stuffing my face. In an effort to slow down, I say, "Enough about me. How did you end up at Bertram?"

"Well," she begins, "I actually received two scholarships. I got an athletic scholarship to play field hockey, and I also got a music scholarship. I play the violin."

"That's cool. How long you been playing?" I ask, focusing more on her and less on my food.

"Since I was like five. My mom thought it was a good idea for me to learn an instrument. I picked it up pretty fast," she says looking down at her salad.

"That's nothing to be ashamed of. You should be proud."

She looks up. "You think so?"

"Definitely. I can't play anything. I admire anybody that can play an instrument. My mom made me take piano lessons for two years. I was horrible. I could never get my right hand and my left hand to work at the same time."

"The piano is hard to play." Erin gives me a sheepish smile.

"Yeah, but instead of going to lessons, I used to ride my dirt bike on the trails in my neighborhood. It worked until my teacher called my mom and asked her why I hadn't been to lessons in two weeks. My mom told her she thought I was going. So I was big-time-busted, but I guess my mom figured if I was that unhappy about going to lessons, I shouldn't have to do it. She was actually pretty cool about it."

Erin laughs at my story, and I can't help but notice her carefree smile. For an instant, I think about Cindy.

Erin must be able to tell my mind is on something else because she asks, "Penny for your thoughts."

"I was just thinking about my girlfriend back home."

"Oh, you're seeing someone? How long have you guys been going out?" Erin asks, sounding disappointed.

"We've been hanging out for about six months. What about you?"

"It seems like I don't have a lot of time for boyfriends, with sports and the violin and all. Plus, I was in the school play."

"You act too?"

"Yeah, I love it. One of my friends suggested we try out for the spring musical together. The play was *Fiddler on the Roof*. Apparently the matchmaker didn't make me a match," she laughs.

I smile back pretending to know what she's talking about.

"Yeah, so what about you and your girl?" Erin asks, moving her salad around her plate.

"Well, we promised to keep in touch. I imagine we'll both be busy. She's a cheerleader, and that takes up a lot of her time. I know it'll be harder once school starts."

Erin nods her head like she gets it. "Well, if she means enough to you, you'll find a way. If it's meant to be, it'll be."

"Yeah, I guess you're right. It's just hard being away from home. I miss my friends. I feel like everything I worked for was for nothing."

Erin looks me in the eye. "You know, life is weird that way. But I bet you'll find that you're here for a reason. You don't know what that reason is, yet. It's like the forces of the universe, stuff we're not supposed to understand. I'm here because I want to go to Julliard and eventually play first chair for the New York Symphony. I figure Bertram gives me the best opportunity to do that. I feel lucky to be here."

I let what Erin said sink in. "I never really looked at it that way. I've been so busy being pissed at my mom for sending me here, I never thought about the opportunities that might be here. I've never really been a very good student. I never even opened a book at Cedarville."

"I can promise you that you'll have plenty of reading to do here," Erin says.

Erin and I talk for two hours, and it seems like ten minutes. And once we get started, there is not a moment of awkward silence. She makes me feel comfortable, but all the talk about school is making me nervous. I have been so focused on football, I haven't even thought about school. I look at Erin. In fact, I can't stop looking at her. "I had a really great time. Maybe we could do this again," I shyly suggest.

Erin glances at me with dark brown eyes. "Yeah, that sounds cool. This week is pretty busy. I have a team meeting tomorrow night, and Wednesday I have a scrimmage. Thursday might be a good day."

"Thursday's good. I have a scrimmage Friday night."

"Thursday it is."

We get up from our table, and I walk Erin back to her dorm. When we arrive at the front of her dorm, she leans toward me and gives me a hug. I am not expecting it, but it is a welcome, friendly hug.

"So, I'll see you Thursday?" Erin asks.

"Yeah. Good luck in your scrimmage."

"Thanks."

I stand outside her dorm and watch her as she opens the door and goes inside. Just the way she moves gives me an energy I have never really felt before. It isn't like getting fired up for a football game. I feel happy—completely alive. Am I in love?

Chapter 14

August 26th

Today at football practice, for the first time in my life, I have a hard time focusing on football. It's like I'm in a trance. My mind keeps drifting from practice to last night's dinner with Erin. I keep seeing her face, her body, and those legs. I'm literally thrown back into reality in our defensive practice when I get absolutely laid out by the offensive tackle on the scout team. I see the guard double on our nose guard with the center, but I don't react in time. If you don't fill the hole on the trap, the tackle comes down on you like a thundering mountain. Most offensive tackles weigh about 250 or 260 pounds in high school. Steve Simms is 270 pounds of flesh and only a sophomore. Needless to say, his hit rockets me off my feet and sends me flying, much to the enjoyment of the scout offense. Everyone starts cheering for Steve.

Coach Kaplan comes over and helps me to my feet. "You all right Morris?"

I adjust my helmet so I'm not looking out my ear hole. "Yeah, I'm okay. I just didn't read the trap block."

"That's not like you. What's on your mind?" he asks knowingly.

"Nothing. I just didn't react in time." I re-snap my chinstrap.

Coach Kaplan looks me over and says, "Don't let it happen again."

"I won't."

He slaps me on the back of the helmet. "Good idea. Simms 'bout broke you in half."

And with that, my thoughts about Erin are put on hold. I know that for my own safety I need to concentrate on what's going on in practice. I finish practice with a few solid tackles and an interception. Coach Kaplan, with his clipboard inside his folded arms, gives me an approving nod. I hope I'm back in his good graces. After practice, I walk back to my dorm around three o'clock. As soon as my head hits the pillow, I'm fast asleep. I crash for two hours. Double sessions are bearable, but they definitely take their toll. I'm glad that I'm able to get in a solid power nap before dinner. I wake up and find Sean reading a book next to me.

"Hey, you want to get some dinner?" he asks.

"Yeah, that sounds great. I'm starving."

* * *

Wednesday and Thursday fly by. They are filled with practices, and sprints, and more sprints, but I feel like I can run forever. I'm looking forward to our first scrimmage on Friday night. All the while, I am anticipating my second meeting with Erin, but I also can't help thinking about Cedarville's first game of the season. After Wednesday's practice, I stop by the field hockey field to watch Erin's scrimmage. I find a spot to watch the scrimmage far enough away from the field to be discreet. She is awesome, fast and aggressive. I watch for about forty-five minutes, and I'm amazed.

Thursday after practice, I meet Erin at the field hockey field.

She jogs off the field and says, "Hey!"

"How's it going?" I ask.

"The last couple of days have been so busy, but our scrimmage was great. I can't wait until our first game. What about you?"

"Only two more days of doubles, and then we have our scrimmage." I let out a deep breath. "But you know what? I can't stop thinking about Cedarville's first game. I miss my friends."

Erin nods her head. "I know where you're coming from. I left great friends back in Columbus, too. It's tough, but it'll get easier once school starts."

"I sure hope so. I met some good guys on the football team, but because I'm playing varsity, I'm stuck between two groups of friends. I play with the seniors, but we're not friends. And the sophomores, I know them better, but I don't play with them. I guess I don't feel like I'm a part of either group. Sometimes, I feel like the guys just like me because I can play."

Erin says, "You don't give yourself enough credit. You're a great guy."

She always seems to say the right thing. I love talking to her because she always makes me feel better. "Hey, thanks for meeting me. I like hanging out with you."

"Yeah," Erin smiles, "hanging out with you is all right."

Back at her dorm, she gives me a big hug. "Good luck in your scrimmage tomorrow. Only three more days until school starts."

I roll my eyes. "Thanks for reminding me."

Erin shrugs her shoulders. "It was inevitable."

"Have a good night," I say.

"Yeah, good night."

As Erin walks away, I can feel this force pulling me toward her.

Halfway back to my dorm, I remember to call Cindy. I hurry my pace and get back to my dorm. I grab my cell phone walk out onto the campus. I dial Cindy's number. The phone rings and rings until I hear her pick up and say, "Hello."

"Hey, it's me."

"Oh, hi," Cindy replies half-heartedly.

"What's the matter?"

"Nothing, why?" she answers back shortly.

"Listen," I begin, "I apologize. I've been busy. When I finally get the time to talk, it's already too late to call. Don't be mad." I can hear her sigh, and she backs off.

"Don't worry. Things have been busy here too, but I miss yew. Why haven't y'all called just to say hello? It only takes a minute."

"I know. I'm sorry. Is everything there okay?" I ask, trying to change the subject.

"Yeah, things have been crazy. It's hard to believe that school starts Monday. My mom and I went shopping today and got some new clothes and school stuff."

"That does sound busy. How's your mom?"

"She's good. How about yer mom?"

It isn't until then that I really think about it, but I haven't heard from my mom since she and Dick dropped me off. "I guess she's okay," I answer. "I haven't talked to her since she left. She and Dick are probably busy selling the house and moving."

"I'm so sorry," Cindy says. She changes the subject. "So, how's your roommate?"

"He's a good guy. We get along okay."

"I'm glad y'all like him. I was worried that y'all would get stuck with some weirdo."

I have been so caught up in my conversations with Erin that my thoughts about Cindy are taking a back seat. We talk for a while; we catch up on all the Cedarville gossip. At ten o'clock, we say goodnight. I know it's late, but I have to call Jack and wish him good luck.

I dial Jack's number, and he answers sounding stuffed up. "Hello."

"You all right?" I ask.

"Billy?"

"Yeah, it's me. Dude, what's up? You sound horrible."
"I don't want to cut you short, but I gotta go."
"What's the matter?"
"Nothing, really, I'm fine."
"I just called to wish you good luck tomorrow night."
"Thanks, man."
"All right," I say as I hang up the phone.

Chapter 15

August 29th 30th

It's Friday and almost my last day of summer vacation. I can hardly believe how much I've gone through during the last month. Despite all that's happened, I feel strong, like I can take on the world. I hang out most of the day, feeling anxious about my first varsity scrimmage. I always get super nervous before games.

We are expected to do summer reading, and the book that is assigned for the sophomore class is *The Things They Carried* by Tim O'Brien. I'm a slow reader, and I'm distracted by thoughts about our scrimmage. I make it through the first five pages and set the book down on my nightstand. Soon after, Sean walks in.

"What's up, man?" he asks.

"Not much, trying to get some reading done. I hate reading."

"You'll like this book. I don't like to read that much either, but it's a Vietnam story with lots of violence. You should give it a shot. Besides, it's due Monday."

"I know. I know," I answer. "I just can't stop thinking about tonight, and I can't stop wondering how Cedarville is going to do tonight. They play a tough schedule this year. They got Cincinnati Moeller tonight."

"Yeah, Moeller is tough. I'm sure your boys will do fine."

I remember my old teammates and how much I miss my friends. I wish I was there, with them, especially Jack.

During the rest of the afternoon, Sean and I hang out, and I try to read some of my book. Finally, I give up, and I go for a walk around the campus. The rolling hills are peaceful; the grass is a bright vibrant green. The trees seem to know that autumn is just around the corner. The smell of football is in the air. I walk the perimeter of the campus, and for the first time since I arrived at Bertram, I notice that it really is an awesome place. The only sound is the birds chirping, maybe because all of the students haven't arrived yet. I walk out to the football field. The field is lined with bright white paint. It almost glows. The stadium is quiet, anticipating greatness. On the football field, I feel like I'm home.

* * *

When I get back to the dorm, I grab my stuff. Sean and I head to the field house so that we can load the bus for our scrimmage. Seniors sit in the back, with Terrance Strong. The juniors come next, and the front of the bus is filled with sophomores. I sit next to Sean. I put my headphones on, and I start listening to some Limp Bizkit: *It's my way, my way or the highway.* By the time we arrive at the public school down the road, I am buzzing with adrenaline.

After we warm up, we start the scrimmage on defense. Hudson High School has an offensive line that averages 260 pounds. They are big, strong, and I quickly discover, fast. When the ball is first snapped, it seems like everything is kicked into fast forward. Practice was one thing, but during the scrimmage, everything seems like a blur. The jump from freshman football to varsity football is insane, super-fast. Because it's a scrimmage, their offense runs ten plays in a row. I feel lost, like I have never played the game before. I think to myself, maybe I am not cut out for varsity football.

Terrance comes up behind me and hits my shoulder pads. I turn around, and he grabs my face mask. Looking into my eyes, into my soul, he says, "Hey, Morris. What the hell you doing? You haven't made a play yet. Why don't you show us what you Cedarville boys are all about? I know you got more game than that."

The Cedarville boys—the thought of all my friends back home gets me fired up. I promised not let them down. I finish the first series and hold my own. By the second set of ten plays, I have adjusted to the speed of the game. On the first three plays, I make two solo tackles and have an assist. I even step in front of a tight-end dump pass and make an interception. I am cheered by new teammates, led by Terrance Strong, and I start to feel like I belong.

After the scrimmage, Coach Carlson comes up to me and says, "You did a nice job out there today. I'm real proud of you. Just keep up the good work, and don't let your head get big. Big egos are the death of good athletes."

Sean and I talk about the scrimmage on the way home. He got in and played some nose guard, and I got to run the ball with the second string offense. I even scored a touchdown. When the busses pull onto the long driveway at Bertram, I am glad to be back and have my first varsity experience under my belt. But I am dying to find out how Cedarville did in their first official game. When I get back, I grab my cell phone to call Jack and Cindy. It's only ten o'clock, but neither one of them answers. Frustrated, I try calling a few more times. I can't get ahold of either one of them. So, I get into bed anxious to see tomorrow's paper in the library. I will be the first one there to grab the sports page.

* * *

My alarm goes off at seven in the morning. I throw on some sweat pants and my tattered Cincinnati Bengal's hat and walk to the library where I find Saturday's paper on the shelf. I search through it looking for the sports page. I can't find it. Discouraged, I look around the library, only to find Erin sitting in a chair in the corner of the room, glancing over the top of Saturday's sports page.

"Are you looking for this?" she mocks. She is wearing her field hockey warm-ups and baseball hat, looking cute as hell.

"Yes, yes I am," I answer willing to play along.

"How much is it worth to you?" she teases.

"Anything you want," I promise.

She smiles and continues, "Looks like your Cedarville boys are a team to be reckoned with. They pounded the number two ranked team in the state, and they're only division four."

My eyes widen. "Really? Can I see that?"

Erin hands me the paper, and sure enough, Cedarville did win 28-7.

THE DAYTON FLYER

High School Football: WEEK 1

The Cedarville Comets started their season with an impressive 28-7 win over #2 state ranked Cincinnati Moeller. The offense was led by sophomore tailback Jack Thompson. Thompson, who was moved from the fullback position, ran like a man possessed. He carried the ball 24 times for 220 yard and three touchdowns. By the end of the night Moeller didn't even want to try and tackle him. The final score was a pass from senior quarterback Danny Towers to Woody Fletcher. Towers finished the night 18 for 24 for 260 yards. The Comets totaled over 500 yards in total offense. The defense shut down Moeller, who only scored one touchdown late in the fourth quarter. Cedarville looks forward to their next game against cross-town rival Tipp City.

Jack never mentioned that Coach Murphy moved him from fullback to tailback. He probably didn't want me to feel bad. I can't believe I'm missing all of this. I'm supposed to be there.

"Are you okay?" Erin asks.

"Yeah, I'm fine. I wish that I was a part of that team." I point to the article in the paper. "It was more than a team to me."

"Don't be upset. There's nothing you can do about it. You're here, and they're there. Don't have any regrets." She shakes her head. "You'll be sorry if you do."

I look up at Erin and think about what she said. I don't know how to feel, but I know that what she said makes sense. The reality is that I'm at Bertram, whether I like it or not. I try to convince myself that if I work hard and do the best that I can, everything will be fine. "You know what?" I say to Erin. "You're right. I'm going to do my best." I fold the newspaper in half.

Erin takes the paper out of my hand. "Now you're talking. What do you say we get some breakfast and celebrate that awesome interception you had in your scrimmage?"

I do a double take and look at Erin. "How did you know about my interception?"

"Mary Jo, one of my girlfriends on the field hockey team, has a car. Her boyfriend is Mike Giffin. You probably know him. He's your starting quarterback. Mary Jo was going to go the scrimmage because it was so close by, and I asked her if I could go."

I must be smiling from ear to ear because Erin just laughs.

"Hey, thanks for coming. I appreciate it."

"Well, maybe there's another reason you ended up at Bertram, other than football." She grabs my hat off my head and runs. I chase after her, and I am surprised to find that I have a hard time catching up. We race to the cafeteria for some breakfast and to talk about the scrimmage and my first varsity football game, which was less than one week away.

Erin reminds me, "School's only two days away. Did you do your summer reading?"

"I don't like to read," I say, chomping down on some pancakes.

"You might want to think about starting off on the right foot."

"Thanks for the advice, but I think I'll be okay."

We sit for about twenty minutes, hanging out and talking until Erin says, "I have some things I need to get done. I have a scrimmage tomorrow evening, but I'll see you in school on Monday."

"Okay, I'll see you later." I stop her and say, "Hey, thanks for the good advice."

Erin gets up from the table. "Don't go soft on me, Billy Morris. You've got some football to play and a book to read."

I take another bite of my pancakes, and with a full mouth I say, "Book? What book?"

Chapter 16

September 1ˢᵗ The first day of school

English is my first class of the day. Walking down the hallway, I'm relieved to see familiar faces from the football team. It definitely makes things easier. I'm even more excited when I see Erin walking toward the same classroom. She catches my eye and says, "Hey, how's it going?"

"Okay, I guess."

"Did you finish reading?" Erin asks.

"I got through the first couple of chapters," I admit.

"Seriously?" I can hear the disappointment in her voice.

"In Cedarville, I never had to read. I just didn't do it."

Erin has a look of frustration. "Come on, we better get to class."

We take our seats next to each other in the back of the room. As soon as we sit down, the teacher comes in. The loud talking among the students dwindles to one or two random conversations.

The teacher waits until everyone is quiet and introduces himself. "My name is Mr. Tanner, and I will be your English teacher this year. This is tenth grade English, just in case anyone is not sure they're in the right place."

After he introduces himself, he moves around the room like a drill sergeant inspecting his troops. His steel blue eyes are intimidating. It's like he can look right through you. He has everyone introduce themselves to the rest of the class. When it comes to me, I say my name and where I'm from. I feel like all eyes are on the new kid.

Mr. Tanner assigns seats. His excitement spreads through the room when he starts class with a discussion about *The Things They Carried*. "Tim O'Brien's writing is as authentic as it comes, from first hand experiences. Because I fought in Vietnam, this unit is important to me on a personal level." I feel like he's going to bring the intensity of the battlefield right into our classroom.

Mr. Tanner asks, "Can anyone shed some light on this summer's reading assignment? What did the book tell you about how soldiers felt about being in Vietnam? How did those feeling change after their first couple weeks in country? Let me see here." He scans his seating chart. "Mr. Morris?"

My paperback is neatly placed on the upper right hand corner of the desk, without any sign of use. I look up, not believing the chances of him calling on me, and respond, "I, uh, did not do the reading."

There is a chuckle from some of the students around me. Clearly, I am the dumb jock. I try to redirect the class's attention. "I think the girl in the back of the room knows the answer." Miss Know-it-all waves her hand violently in the back row.

After giving me a penetrating stare, Mr. Tanner shifts his attention to the other side of the room and calls on another student. During the rest of the class, I slouch down in my chair, trying to remain out of sight. My first day of school is off to a miserable start. I think about my mother for getting me into this situation. Mr. Tanner's class seems like an eternity. When class winds down, Mr. Tanner looks directly at me and says, "There will be a written test over the material during tomorrow's class."

So now I have football practice and an entire novel to read . . . tonight.

Mr. Tanner dismisses the class. As the class filters out of the room, he pulls me aside and says, "Mr. Morris, I want a word with you." When the last student leaves the classroom, Mr. Tanner closes the door. He moves into my personal space. He towers over me. He looks at me and says in a low and serious tone, "Mr. Morris, I don't know why your reading isn't done, but know this—I can be your best ally or your worst enemy. See to it that you do the work in my class." He moves his face only inches from mine, and his voice thunders when he says, "I don't want to have this conversation again. Is that clear?"

I look at Mr. Tanner wide-eyed. I don't know what to say. I've never had a teacher talk to me like that. I manage to get out a, "Yes, sir. I'll do the work."

As the day wears on, I discover that Bertram is more of a challenge than I ever could have imagined. My second period is French class. I took French for three years. I thought I knew the language pretty well, but the second year French teacher doesn't say one word in English. I'm in way over my head in that class. From there, I head to Art class, not one of my stronger subjects. Our art teacher, Mr. McDaniel, explains that we have to draw a landscape of the campus. We sit outside with our drawing pencils and these giant boards. At one point, Mr. McDaniel looks over my shoulder. He pulls his long black hair into a ponytail and asks me, "What is it that you got there?"

I try to explain, "Um, that's that tree over there, and that's that building."

"I see," he says. At least he seems patient, friendly, like a hippy from the 60's.

My schedule reads that my fourth period is a *free period*. I don't even know what a free period is. At Cedarville, we had study halls. I start walking around the campus to ask someone what a free period is. There is a student center where some students hang out. Students are dispersed around campus lying on the lawn, playing Frisbee, reading books. It's the weirdest thing. I finally get the nerve to ask a student who is sitting on the lawn doing some math homework. It looks like Algebra.

He explains, "During your free period, your time is your time, to do what you want. Some kids hang out. I try to get as much of my homework done so I don't have to do it at after school."

The first thing that pops into my mind is reading *The Things They Carried*. Then, I feel a tap on my shoulder. It's Erin. Man, am I glad to see her.

"Hey, are you making it through the day?" she asks.

"I guess it's harder than I thought it would be. These classes are impossible."

"Yeah, I've been pretty busy too, but I'm excited," Erin explains.

"What are you so excited about?"

"I just had my music class. My teacher is amazing. I think that she can teach me a lot about the violin. It's kinda why I'm here."

"That's cool. But I just have one question, what's the deal with free periods?" I laugh.

"Yeah, awesome, huh? Maybe we should get some reading done."

We find a spot under a big maple tree in front of the large white house that serves as the campus cafeteria. I read my book while Erin does some of her Spanish homework. Surprising even myself, I manage to read a few chapters of the novel before Erin and I go to lunch together. Despite the fact that I hate reading, I find myself getting interested in the story.

My afternoon is filled with three classes. I have Geometry, where I have to learn the first five theorems and do twenty sample problems for homework. My science class is Biology, where we study the anatomy of the frog. I have to read chapters one to three. Tomorrow we get to begin dissecting our own frog. Lucky us. The last class of the day is World History. Our homework is to read the first two chapters in our textbook. The teachers seem pretty nice, but Bertram is very different from Cedarville. The teachers are more like professors, and the students never goof off. The students are focused, dedicated. I walk from my last class of the day toward the gym to get changed for football practice. On my way over to the gym, I see Erin and catch up to her.

"I see you survived," she jokes.

"Barely," I respond. "I didn't know this was the Ivy League."

"You'll adjust."

"I hope so. Hey, I gotta run to practice. I'll talk to you later?"

Erin stops me and says, "I can help you study for the summer reading test if you want."

"I'm in. How about the library at eight?"

Erin looks back over here shoulder and says, "I'll see you then."

Monday's practice is light. We do some jogging and watch some film of our first opponents, the Chardon Hilltoppers, the Division II State runner up from last year. I try to focus on practice, but my mind is filled with my first day of school and my encounter with Mr. Tanner.

I have only read through the first eight chapters of the book, only seventeen more to go. Our practice ends early, so I go to my dorm and try to get as much reading done as I can. I grab some food at the cafeteria and make my way to the library to meet Erin.

Erin is in the back of the library in her usual casual warm-up attire with her cherry-red Ohio State baseball hat.

"Hey, Billy," she flirts. "Are you ready to get to work?"

"Yeah," I reply, "I got some of the reading done after practice. I only have about ninety pages to go."

We find a study table, and we talk a little bit about the book. With Erin's help and after being threatened by Mr. Tanner, I've never been more focused. Apparently, intimidation is a very effective teaching tool. Erin's explanation makes things easier to understand. We read the last five chapters out loud to each other. It takes us almost an hour, but I feel ready for my test the next day.

"You have a great reading voice," Erin comments. "You should join the debate team or something."

I laugh. "Maybe I should just worry about passing this test tomorrow."

Erin nods her head. "Yeah, you're right, baby steps."

"What do you have the rest of the week?" I ask Erin.

"Well, let's see. I have a violin recital on Thursday. And, oh yeah, I'm going to try to make it to your game on Friday. Mary Jo said that she is going to drive."

"That's cool. I'll go to your recital on Thursday."

"It's a deal."

"Hey, thanks for helping me with all of this school stuff. You know you don't have to."

"I know I don't have to, maybe we'll both do better by helping each other."

* * *

Tuesday morning, Mr. Tanner hands me the test. I take it and answer each question knowing that my responses are correct. It is the beginning of my new approach to school. My week is a mixture of classes, practices, Erin's game, and her violin recital.

On Thursday night, I go to Erin's recital. I settle in the back of the auditorium and look at the program. Across from Erin's name it reads: *Bach's Lullaby*. I never had an appreciation for classical music or the violin until I see Erin alone on that stage, under the spotlight. Each note is distinct, perfect. Her brown hair glistens and blends perfectly with the wood of the violin. In the back of the auditorium, I'm swept away by the music, riding on each note. I wonder how I could be so lucky to have met a girl like Erin.

Friday morning rolls around, the day of my first varsity football game under the lights. I try to focus in my classes, but I can't. I'm nervous as hell.

Chapter 17

Friday September 5th

I've got a ball of rage in the pit of my stomach, and I'm ready to explode. I'm standing in front of the mirror in Chardon's visiting team's locker room. The eyeblack under my eyes completes my gladiator's uniform. My helmet is gray with red wings on either side. I proudly wear my favorite number, 22. I have made my transformation into a warrior. I'm nervous, but I know that no one has worked harder for this opportunity.

I tape my wrists with athletic tape from the trainer, my pre-game ritual. Sean walks up to me and pounds his fists on my shoulder pads. "Are you ready?" he shouts all fired up.

I just nod my head.

Bertram has prepared for bigger games than this one, but to me, it's the biggest game of my life.

Coach Carlson calls the team together, and we huddle in the middle of the locker room. We are a team.

"No fear," Coach Carlson begins, "we have spent the last few weeks preparing for this. Have no fear, because preparation and dedication erase all that. Your teammates erase all that. The person next to you will not let you down, and you will not let them down. Pick each other up. Be relentless.

Be courageous. Play together and play hard. Make sure when this game is over, you have left everything on the field. Men, if you do that, I promise you, you will be victorious. This is when all the hard work you have invested since the beginning of January, over the summer, and the last few weeks of double sessions pays off. It's time to withdraw that investment. Believe that your hard work will be rewarded today. Captains, get everyone together, and LET'S GET IT DONE. LET'S BRING HOME A VICTORY."

A chill shoots through my body. The captains lead our team in a prayer, the "Our Father." I hear the cleats scraping along the floor of the locker room as we get into two lines side by side. Sean and I are partners. As we exit the locker room, I slide my helmet over my head like Russell Crow in *Gladiator*, ready for battle.

When we get to the corner of the end zone, we jog to the fifty yard line and get into our stretching positions. During our warm-up routine, the captains go to the fifty-yard line for the coin toss. The referee uniforms glow bright white, brand new for the first game of the season. Terrance returns to the team to tell us that we won the toss and deferred to the second half. We will be starting on defense, but first we will have to kick off. I'm a headhunter on the kickoff team, and my job is to bust the blocking wedge.

I slap my hands on my thigh pads and dig my cleats into the ground. The kickoff turns end over end and is caught by their return man, who is also their starting tailback, Scott Thomas. The scouting reports say he isn't big, only 5'6", but he is an All-State track athlete. I run full speed toward the mass of bodies and hurl myself at the first man leading the wedge. The popping of the pads echoes throughout the stadium, and I destroy the first man; the rest of the wedge disintegrates. Sean comes in from the side and puts a solid hit on Scott, and he takes him down. The first defense sprints out onto the field. My left forearm and hand are scraped up, but it doesn't faze me. I love the contact, the battle, the high.

I take my place as the inside linebacker in our base 52 defense. I make calls to my defensive lineman, "Stick 52, Ram, Ram," calling a slant to the right. Their quarterback, an All-State basketball player, comes to the line of scrimmage and looks over the defense. I peer into his eyes from behind my facemask. He seems calm, relaxed. The fire in my gut burns hotter.

He shouts out the signals, "BLUE 20. BLUE 20 SET, HUT." The ball is snapped. I read the guard doubling on the nose; the play is a fullback trap. I shoot the gap and meet the fullback head on. The contact is solid as my shoulder rams into his thigh. I wrap his legs and lift, driving him into the hard-packed earth. I hear him groan on impact. I feel a shot of adrenaline. I no longer feel human. Mobbed by my team, they slap me on the helmet in celebration of the big hit.

Coach Kaplan signals in defenses to Marcus Tyler and shouts encouragement. He is completely engaged on the sideline with his headphones and clipboard. He barks in the referee's ear, "Watch the holding! Their left tackle is holding our defensive end! Throw the flag! Do your job!"

On the next play, the quarterback drops back and breaks contain. He begins to scramble and heads for our sidelines. I take a perfect angle and run him down for a two yard loss. Marcus slaps me on the helmet and shouts, "Way to go, baby!"

On third down and twelve, their quarterback drops back and throws a ball that sails over the head of his wide receiver. Chardon lines up to punt on fourth down. Terrance is the deep man, and I stand ten yards in front of him as his lead blocker.

"You ready, Morris?" he yells. "Let's make it happen!"

"Let's do it!" I shout back.

Terrance receives the punt and follows my lead. I throw a punishing block on the first man, and he makes two people miss, almost breaking it for a touchdown. Chardon will have their hands full containing Terrance Strong.

Even though Chardon has a solid returning team, Terrance runs and jumps over and through the Hilltopper defense. On the few occasions that his wiry and elusive frame does not make the corner on a sweep, he lowers his shoulder and punishes the defender, surprising them with his strength. On one play, he starts running to the right, cuts all the way back across the field, and ends up on the left side of the field, in the end zone, for a touchdown. I'm glad Terrance is on our team. By the end of the night, Chardon is fighting with each other, pointing fingers. Terrance finishes the night with 189 yards rushing on only 18 carries. He scores three touchdowns. Our defense doesn't give up a single point. Chardon only manages to cross the fifty yard line one time. We win 21-0.

Coach Carlson brings us together in the locker room, a scene not that different from the beginning of the game. He says, "Even though we are a smaller division school, we took it to 'em. We played together as a team. Every aspect of our game was solid. We were better prepared, in better shape, hungrier. Men, this is just the beginning. Game one is over. Enjoy it. We'll be back to work on Monday for game two. Remember, one game at a time."

It is amazing the power that words can have. Coach Carlson makes me feel important, proud, and lucky to be a part of this team.

In my first varsity game as a starting sophomore, I have eight tackles, one sack, and an interception. But it isn't the stats that make me feel good, the best part of the game is the feeling I get inside, the adrenaline, the natural high. I take it all in: playing under the lights, the smell of the grass, the crowd, the feeling of being invincible, the opportunity to be a part of a team, a family.

It's only been three weeks since I left Cedarville, but already, because of being on the football team at Bertram, I feel like I belong. In the middle of all that excitement, I wonder how my old teammates did in their second game.

I regret that I am not with them, but the pain of that situation is dwindling, and my closeness with my teammates from Bertram is growing.

As the school bus rolls out of the parking lot, I think about what football gives to me: the opportunity to play a sport that I love, bond with my teammates, and be part of something that is meaningful. I'm proud to be part of this team, defining my character, finding my place in the world.

Chapter 18

September 6th

I jump out of bed and race to the library to get Saturday's paper. I find Erin waiting for me.

She says, "I figured I'd find you here, wanting to know how Cedarville did last night. By the way, great game! You were awesome!"

I step back and look at Erin. "I'm glad you were there."

"You did a good job," she says as she hands me the sports page. It's already turned to the article about Cedarville's second game.

THE DAYTON FLYER

High School Football: WEEK 2

The Cedarville Comets increased their record to 2-0 by overpowering Tipp City 42-7. Once again Cedarville was led by the hard-running and tackling of sophomore tailback-linebacker Jack Thompson. Thompson scored four rushing touchdowns for the Comets. He ran for 195 yards on 30 carries. He was the workhorse for the Comets. On defense he dominated with 14 tackles. Jimmy Towers continued to demonstrate his strength at the quarterback position by throwing for 280 yards and two touchdowns. Tipp City never got in the game. The Comets came out pounding the ball. Led by a strong and fast offensive line, Thompson punished would-be-tacklers and scored three of his four touchdowns in the first half. Cedarville will face Dayton Dunbar next Friday night.

I looked at Erin and say, "Man, Jack is playing great. I gotta call him."

"You must be excited for him."

"I just wish I was with him—in the backfield. We should be playing together."

Erin points at me. "You should call him?"

"I'm going to try right now. You want to meet later for lunch?"

"I'll meet you at noon in front of the cafeteria!"

I grab my phone and head out onto the campus. I dial Jack's number and listen to the ringing as I walk toward the football field.

Jack answers. "Hello."

"Hey man, it's me, Billy."

"It seems like I haven't talked to you forever. How you doing?" Jack asks.

It is good to hear Jack's voice. "I'm doing okay. Last night was amazing. My first varsity football game! It wasn't how I pictured it. I mean, I pictured it with you guys, wearing the blue and gold."

"I know what you mean. It's not the same without you."

Jack's words cut into me. It hits me how much I really miss being there, how much I miss my best friend.

"I've been reading the sports page. You have like five touchdowns already! Sounds like all that hard work is paying off."

"Yeah, man, it's an awesome feeling, running into the end zone, looking up at all the fans. I was nervous before the game started, but once I scored that first touchdown, it was like I was in control. I felt like no one could tackle me, like I was unstoppable. Everyone on the team is starting to come together."

A lump sits in my throat. "How is everything else?"

I hear a deep breath on the other end of the line.

"You doing okay?" I ask again.

His excited tone turns quiet. "Things at home are kinda tough. My old man got a DUI last Friday after the football game, spent the weekend in jail. He's meeting with his lawyer today. He's been drinking every night. Last Thursday before our first game, he came home from the bar drunk, pulled me out of bed, and started pushing me around. I think he bruised one of my ribs. I could barely breathe. I wasn't going play last week."

"But you did."

"Yeah, I took it all out on Moeller. I punished 'em. Those dudes wanted nothing to do with me. I figure for every punch my dad dished out, I would make those guys pay. I was like possessed or something. Even coach Murphy asked me if I was all right."

"What did you tell him?"

"I told him I was all fired up, first varsity game and all that. He ate it up."

"What can I do?" I ask.

"It'll work itself out."

"Are you sure?"

"You got enough going on," Jack reminds me.

"You know, I haven't even talked to my mom since she dropped me off, over three weeks ago," I say, realizing how long it's been.

"I saw her and Dick just the other day. They sold the house. She's moving down to South Carolina next week. She said she's been calling you, leaving messages on your phone. She says you never answer it."

"I don't feel like talking to her."

Jack changes the subject. "How tough are those boys at Bertram?"

"Some of the guys are really tough. They're from all over; some are on scholarships for music or sports. Most of them transferred here as freshman. Some are from inner city Cleveland, bad dudes, hard hitters, and fast. They play the game like it's supposed to be played. Terrance Strong is the real deal, talks about going pro all the time, already has college recruiters coming to the games. Bobby Bowden wrote him a five page hand-written letter telling him how much he wanted him at Florida State."

"No kidding," Jack sounds excited. "Bobby Bowden? That's awesome."

"It's pretty cool. This whole group of seniors is like professionals, you know, the way they prepare for games and things like that. It's easy to see how they won State last year."

Jack jumps in, "Speaking of that, did you know we could play in the playoffs? Cedarville and Bertram are in the same division! Could you imagine playing against each other! I would crush you."

"Yeah, right. I would knock you down!" I say.

"Whatever, but just think, it could happen."

"Well, we'll see. The season just started. The playoffs are a long ways away."

"It's something to think about." Jack says.

"Yeah, you're right." Talking to Jack makes me feel better. "Can we do a better job of keeping in touch? If you ever need to talk to somebody about your dad or anything, call me. Don't go it alone man; you don't have to. That's what friends are for."

"I know, things have been nuts. Leigh and I fight all the time. She says that I'm always pissed off. We got in this huge fight after last night's game. I got all drunk at Danny Tower's house. His parents were out of town, so we went there after the game. She saw me all wasted and said I was acting like an idiot. She says I'm changing, that I'm not the guy I used to be. She's been threatening to break up with me. I don't care what she does. Anymore, I got enough to deal with."

"She cares about you."

"The only thing I've got in my life right now is football. It's my outlet. It's the only place I can go to get away from all of this. When I'm on the field, I become someone else. You know, I put that helmet on, and all of sudden, I'm in control."

"I know how you feel. It's the only time I feel like I belong here. It's the only time I feel normal." I think to myself, and then say, "Until I met this girl."

"Oh, yeah. Who is she?"

"Erin. She's got brown hair. She's all tan, perfect smile. She plays the violin, sings, acts. She's on the field hockey team."

"What about Cindy? She's been asking about you."

"I don't know what to do. I don't know how to tell her."

"You have to tell her how you feel. It's your life man. If you drag it out, it's only going to make things worse."

"I know. You're right, but that doesn't make it any easier. I don't want to hurt her."

"You're just hurting her worse by not telling her how you feel. She'll get over it."

"I don't think she would understand the things I've been through. Erin is amazing. She always says the right things. When I talk to her, I feel like we've known each other forever. She knows everything about me, and she still doesn't think I'm crazy."

"Not many girls would put up with either one of us."

"You got that right. I'll figure it out. I won't drag things out."

"Listen man, my dad's going to be back soon, and I don't want to be here when he gets back. I'm going to meet Leigh. Good job last night."

"Yeah, you too. I'll talk to you soon. Don't be a stranger, like the rest of the guys back in Cedarville. You know I haven't talked to a single one of them."

"It's tough finding out who your real friends are."

We say goodbye, and I hang up the phone. Standing way out on the soccer fields, I start thinking about how I've lost contact with so many of my other friends: Woody, Chris, Pat, and Tombo. I think about how fast my good friends slipped away. I think about Tombo and watching *Caddy Shack* until the sun came up down in his basement. I think about Woody Fletcher and the good times we used to have riding our bikes into town and buying burgers with spare change at Mill's diner. I think about Chris and playing little league baseball, singing songs in his mom's mini-van on the way home. When I was in eighth grade, I figured I had twenty best friends. By ninth grade, I had maybe ten good buddies. And here I am, a year later, with only one person I can rely on and call my friend.

Chapter 19

September 7th and 8th

I check the messages on my phone and discover that my mother has left five messages since I arrived at Bertram. The messages are short, but I can tell by the tone of her voice that she is concerned about me. She left a number where I can reach her. She and Dick found a temporary apartment and are looking for a new house in South Carolina. She said that the weather is beautiful, and she can't wait until I come and visit.

I'm not interested in my mother's invitation. I feel a resentment that I find hard to describe. There she is living her life, and here I am living my life, trying to make the best out of my situation at Bertram. Everyday, I miss my friends and my old life in Cedarville. There was so much I had planned for, had worked for. I try to understand what I did to deserve this. I resent my mom and Dick. Hell, I'm angry at the world!

As I play my mom's last message, Sean comes into the dorm and sits down. He looks tired, bummed.

"What's up?" I ask.

"It's nothing, really," Sean says, plopping his head back on his pillow.

"Dude, you look miserable."

Sean takes a deep breath. "I thought this was going to be a new beginning for me."

"What are you talking about? You've been doing awesome. You got some varsity time at nose guard."

"You don't understand. My dad can be a real jerk sometimes. He sent me here with all these expectations. He's been telling all the coaches and parents that I am going to be the next Terrance Strong. He puts so much pressure on me, I feel like I'm going to burst."

"Terrance, huh. Those are big shoes. Why's he doing that?"

"I don't know. He picked up and moved our whole family here from Tipp City. He thought this would be my opportunity to get a scholarship somewhere. You know, play college ball. He's a high school teacher and doesn't make much money. He said I would have to pay for college on my own."

I can see how Sean has changed since he arrived. He's not as friendly, less patient. Sean is a good athlete, but he's flighty. So the coaches haven't put him in an important position, a position where he has to make a lot of decisions. I guess that's why they put him at nose guard. All he has to do is try to beat the center and get into the backfield. With his speed and strength, he's a great nose guard.

Sean looks at me with tired eyes. "What am I going to do?"

"It's only your sophomore year. This team is mostly juniors and seniors. There are only three starters that are not seniors. You'll get your chance."

Sean sits up and says, "I wish my dad saw it that way. He pisses me off. I wish he could see that I was doing my best and stop putting so much pressure on me. Some of the players are even starting to give me a hard time. They've been calling me Terrance, things like that."

"I didn't realize things were so tough." Even though we are roommates, Sean rarely shared the things that were going on in his life. I tell him, "Things will get better."

* * *

Things for Sean don't get better. In fact, they get a whole lot worse. After practice on Monday, the seniors get him. They start their ritual of taping unsuspecting sophomores. They steal the white athletic tape from the trainer, about ten roles. They gang up on one sophomore and wrap him up like a mummy.

Today, it's Sean, led by none other than Terrance Strong. The hazing ritual is on its way before I get back to the locker room, which is about a half-mile from the field. I walk into the locker room and see six seniors carrying a mummy into the showers. I hear Sean yelling, "PUT ME DOWN. ASS-HOLES." Sean tries to fight back. He kicks and shouts, without any luck. The other sophomores skip showers and get out, ignoring the yells for help, saving themselves.

I run toward the showers where I am met by half of the offensive line. Andy Heyman puts out his hand and says, "This ain't your problem, Morris. Just go about your business."

I try to get to Sean, who is hung up on a towel hook. He is suspended a good twelve inches from the floor of the shower. The seniors are writing on the tape in red marker. I try to get to Sean and help him. The linemen stand in the way. Because I'm outmatched, I reluctantly go back to my locker. Eventually, they take Sean off the hook and carry him to the gymnasium. I follow behind them.

A few of the seniors slide him into the gym. Sean manages to get up and hop out of the gym because his feet are still tied together. There are tears running down his face, fury burning in his eyes.

I run over to Sean and start removing the tape. He pushes me away. "Get off me!" he grunts. "Don't touch me!"

"I was out at the field. I tried to help."

"Leave me the hell alone," he mutters while pulling the tape from the hair on his head and legs. The tape pulls hard on the hair, and he is shaking.

If his father only knew that he brought all of this onto his son, if he only knew. This wasn't even Sean's fault. He's a good guy, who works hard and keeps his mouth shut, tries to do his best. His father pushes him too hard and runs his mouth in the stands to the other parents. I can't even begin to understand the anger and embarrassment that Sean must feel. He grabs his equipment and walks out the back door of the locker room.

* * *

The next day at practice, the team is met with a very different side of Coach Carlson. His eyes narrow and he says, "You guys think you're tough. What was it, ten seniors on one sophomore? Shameful, embarrassing, ridiculous. Is that the way to treat another member of the team? Is that the way to be a team?"

Coach Carlson knows the seniors are responsible, but he probably isn't sure exactly who participated. He can't suspend the entire senior class, all of which were a part of the assault, including a few of the juniors. "WE ARE A TEAM! WE ARE A TEAM! Those of you who participated in yesterday's hazing should be ashamed. This stops now. If I so much as hear of anything resembling hazing, you will be removed, not just from the team, from Bertram. IS THAT CLEAR!" Coach Carlson's face has turned a dark shade of red.

Everyone responds, "Yes, coach." It's silent except for the dripping water coming from the shower room. Coach's words have sunk in. Many of the seniors have their heads down, realizing they went beyond what they thought was a practical joke.

After practice, Coach Carlson keeps all of the seniors. They start on the goal line with bear crawls. Then every ten yards they get to their feet, and then they do ten grass drills. Four hundred yards and 440 grass drills later, the seniors start to understand what they did was wrong.

After practice, I walk back to the locker room with Sean. He seems to be doing better. I tell him, "Listen man, I'm sorry about yesterday."

"I don't want to hear it Billy. It's not going to be okay. No thanks to you either."

"Come on, man. There was nothing I could do."

"I have to live with this, not you!"

I can see in Sean's eyes that he wants revenge, and he wants nothing to do with me. He doesn't seem to care.

I decide to leave Sean alone. Being roommates with Sean is not going to be easy.

On the way back to the dorm, I run into Erin who has just finished field hockey practice. She jogs over to me with her usual smile. I don't smile back.

"What's the matter?" she asks.

I tell her the whole story about Sean.

"He must be humiliated. He seems like such a good guy."

"Yeah, he really is. I think he just needs some time to get over it."

"Just be his friend. Don't get frustrated if he won't talk to you."

"I think I can do that," I say, relieved to be able to talk to Erin.

"Hey," she says, "don't forget, we have a test tomorrow in English."

"Yeah, I know. I've been studying. I promised Tanner."

I return to my dorm with Erin on my mind. I know that I feel something for her, something I have never felt before. She makes me feel good about myself; she makes me feel alive.

The realization sets in that I have to break up with Cindy. I have to figure out a way to do it. I know she'll be hurt. I walk toward the baseball fields. It is 7:30, and the September sun is still warm. I dial Cindy's number.

"Hello," a quiet voice answers.

"Cindy, hey, it's me Billy."

"Billy, oh my gosh, I was just thinking about yew. I was hoping y'all would call."

This is going to be harder than I thought. It wasn't that long ago that I was convinced that I was falling for Cindy.

Cindy says after my long silence, "Hello? Are yew there? What are y'all doing?"

"Yeah, hey, I'm here. I'm out at the baseball fields. How have you been? How's cheerleading?"

"It's good," Cindy says. "School has been busy with practice and games and all that. I feel like the first few weeks of school have flown by. I'm always thinking about yew, wondering how y'all are doing."

"I'm doing okay. Football's been good. My English teacher almost killed me, and my other classes are impossible. My head has been spinning."

"That does sound tough. School here is good. I have some pretty cool teachers this year. Cheerleading's been awesome."

"That's really good."

"You know, I was thinking that maybe I could come up to see yer first home game this weekend. What do y'all think?" Cindy asks.

"Cindy?" My brain spins.

"Yeah, what's up?"

"I don't think that's such a good idea."

"How come?" she asks, sounding disappointed.

I take a deep breath and look out over the vacant baseball field from my seat, now high on the top row of the bleachers. "You're a great friend, and I want to stay friends. I need to figure some things out."

"Billy, did I do something wrong?"

My heart pounds, and my stomach aches. "I feel like I have too much going on right now. I feel bad when I don't have a chance to call you. I'm really sorry."

"I don't want to lose yew. We can make this work," Cindy says, now sounding more angry than sad.

"Don't be mad. We can still be friends."

"Friends? Y'all have got to be kidding."

"It doesn't have to end this way."

"Y'all want to know something? I thought you were better than that."

"Cindy?"

"I gotta go." She hangs up the phone.

I sit on the bleachers and close my phone. Strangely, it isn't sadness that I feel, but rather, a sense of relief, like a giant burden has been lifted off my shoulders. I won't have to feel guilty about talking to Erin, and I won't feel bad about not calling Cindy. I tell myself that Cindy will be fine, that it will just take some time.

I sit looking down at my phone, and then I dial Jack's number. I hope he's home because I need a good friend to talk to.

"Hello," Jack answers.

"It's me, Billy."

"What's up, bro?"

"I just broke up with Cindy," I say.

"You did what? Unbelievable."

"I know. I feel bad. I'm sure she hates me."

"Don't worry about. She'll be fine."

"I didn't want to hurt her."

"She's cool; she'll get over it." Jack tries to reassure me. "Listen man, you did the right thing. You were just being honest with her."

"Yeah, I guess you're right." I try to change the subject. "So, how are you and things in Cedarville?"

"My old man is out at the bar. He already has that DUI, so now he walks up to the Tavern. He's like the town drunk."

I try to understand his life. I feel bad because I'm not there to help him. "I wish I was there man."

"Yeah, me too. Leigh and I got in another huge fight about my drinking. She told me I'm gonna be just like my old man."

"What did you say to her?"

"I told her she didn't have a clue what my dad was like, and that she should mind her own damn business. I haven't talked to her since. She won't even look at me at school."

"What are you going to do?"

"Don't know."

"She'll get over it."

"It just gets frustrating, everybody talking about my dad. It seems like everyone is making my life, their business. Even Coach Murphy was asking about how I was doing at home."

"Hey, man, don't let that stuff get to you."

"I live with it everyday. Last night the bartender at the Tavern called here and told me to come get my dad because he could barely stand up, on a Monday night."

"My only advice is do the best you can at school and at football, and just hope things work out for your dad."

"Yeah, I just wish I could help him. He means well; he just doesn't get it, always pissed off at the world. He doesn't know how to talk to people, and since my mom left, I think he feels like he doesn't have anything to live for."

I called Jack feeling sorry for myself and about Cindy and my life at Bertram. What I didn't expect is feeling bad for him and his situation. It seems like football is the only thing positive in his life, and despite everything that is going on with him, he's there for me, willing to listen.

"Don't worry about things with Cindy," Jack replies.

"Thanks."

"Who do you guys play this week?"

It's our first home game; we play Gilmour. It should be interesting. We play our home games on Saturdays at two o'clock."

"Good luck man; get a big hit for me. We play Dunbar. Those kids are fast. Coach Murphy has put in a special defense to try and contain their quarterback. Do you remember him in track last year? He ran the 200 meters in like 22.0 seconds; he's only a junior. He's got a cannon for an arm. And their tailback, Trent Nellums, won the state 100 meter final last year as a junior. They're undefeated."

"If you keep running the way you have been, you guys should be fine. Let me know how things are going with your dad and how things work out with Leigh."

"Yeah, you hang in there too. Let me know how that new girl Erin is. I'm out, Morris."

"Yeah, I'll catch up with you later."

I hang up the phone, and the sun is going down. I feel fortunate to have a friend like Jack. His friendship was something I always took for granted, but now I know how lucky I am.

Chapter 20

September 13th

Saturday morning I make my usual trek to the library to look at the paper and read the article about Cedarville's Friday night game.

THE DAYTON FLYER

High School Football: WEEK 3
The Cedarville Comets found themselves in a dogfight last night against a fast and strong Dayton Dunbar team. Cedarville won the contest in double overtime 28-21. Regulation ended in a 14-14 tie. Trent Nellums led Dunbar with 180 yards rushing on only 20 carries. However, he was outdone by Jack Thompson who was the workhorse for Cedarville and carried the ball 35 times for 225 yards. His powerful running served the Comets well in the overtime period where Dunbar just could not stop him. The 3-0 Comets face Oakwood next week. Dunbar travels to Upper Arlington.

Every time I read about Cedarville, it feels like a piece of me is missing. I was supposed to be a part of that team. Thinking about Cedarville makes it difficult to focus on the game I have to play. And even though I know breaking up with Cindy was the right thing to do, I miss her already. I miss being a part of a team where I know everybody. I miss being home.

I see Sean sitting at the far end of the cafeteria. I grab my breakfast and sit with him. At least he doesn't object to my sitting at his table.

"Cedarville had a big win over Dunbar last night," I tell him.

Sean looks me up and down and then lets out a deep breath. "They did? How did Tipp do last night?"

"They won 21-7 last night against Oakwood. Cedarville plays them next week." I'm glad to bring Sean good news, if it is good news.

"That's cool," Sean says sounding a bit more like his old self.

"Yeah, you excited about playing Gilmour today?"

"As ready as I'm going to be," Sean replies. "I don't feel a part of this team."

"Listen, you have to let that go. Put it behind you. You have to focus on the game, or you're going to get hurt."

"Maybe I should quit," Sean shoots back.

"Show these guys that you're better then that."

"You know, you're the only person I trust around here," he says.

"Show em' that we Dayton boys know how to play ball."

The look on Sean's face begins to change. "You know what, you're right."

We walk to the gym to get our equipment ready for the game. I start my pre-game ritual of walking the campus and doing some light stretching and running. Behind the locker room, there are two acres of open space. In my football pants and my gray t-shirt with cut off sleeves, I begin to put myself in the right frame of mind.

Back at the gym, the trainer is taping ankles while some of the guys shoot baskets in the gym. About two hours before the game, we jog out to the field house and begin our special team warm-up: kicking, punting, and throwing. I work with the punters.

Within a half hour, the Gilmour team pulls up in their school bus. My heart begins to pound, and I am ready for the kickoff.

Terrance comes over to me and says, "You nervous, Morris?"

"Naw," I reply. "I'm good."

"Cuz, I am. I always get nervous before games. I used to let it bother me, until someone told me it was good to be a little bit nervous. It gets you sharp, ready to play."

I come clean and tell Terrance, "Honestly man, I get so nervous before games. Sometimes, I feel like I'm going to puke."

"Hey Morris, it just means you're human. It's a good thing. You just have to channel that energy, make it work for you." Terrance smiles. "You know, I been meaning to tell you, ever since that little fight we got in, I got some respect for you. You know, coming here, not knowing anybody, kicking some ass. You're all good in my book."

"Yeah, you're not so bad yourself."

Kickoff is just ten minutes away when our first string nose guard, John Bates, goes down with a pulled calf muscle during warm-ups. He can barely run. Coach Carlson tells Sean he will be starting at nose guard. I see the determination in Sean's eyes. He will get his chance to prove himself to the team. He comes over and gives me the news. "I'm going to light somebody up today."

Gilmour wins the coin toss, and they decide to receive. We line up our kickoff team. Sean and I are the headhunters. We sprint down the field and destroy the blocking wedge, taking out the first two players. Gilmour has no idea they are going to meet the pent up frustration and rage of Sean Foran. He's in the huddle growling.

On the line of scrimmage, Sean digs his cleats into the ground. The turf flies up behind him. On the first play, he does a swim technique over the center. It is a dive play to their tailback. Sean plants his helmet squarely on the chest of the unsuspecting running back. The force knocks the runner off the ground. He and Sean are both airborne. The loud pop echoes through the stadium. Sean drives the runner into the ground like he is trying to put him six feet under. The players on the defense go to congratulate him on his big hit, but he ignores them. He just returns to the spot of the ball and calls for the defense to huddle up. Everyone just looks at each other. Sean's eyes glaze over. He's in a different place.

By the second quarter, Gilmour's center is shaking. Sean spits on the ball and grunts. He has ten tackles, and they are some of the most violent hits I have ever seen. He's no longer the kid who got taped. He has created his own identity. He is a freaking animal, one that nobody wants to mess with.

We pound Gilmour 35 to 7. Terrance runs like a madman. He scores four touchdowns. Three of them are long runs. One is a seventy-three yard punt return. I have twelve tackles and an interception. While playing tailback, I see Erin in the stands, and I want to show off for her. I score a touchdown late in the fourth quarter.

After the game, Coach Carlson brings the team together in the end-zone. "Men, he begins, "great effort out there today. Rest up tomorrow. We have a light practice on Monday. Remember to get your school work done. And don't forget to be on your best behavior." I look over at Sean and see a look of satisfaction.

After the game, I see Erin standing with a group of her friends. She makes her way through the crowd. I carry my helmet and shoulder pads. The eyeblack is smeared on my face. She comes up and gives me an unexpected kiss on the cheek. "Great game," she says. "Nice touchdown."

"I forgot how much I missed running the ball."

"Yeah, well, awesome job."

"It's nice to know I have someone in my corner."

"Well," Erin laughs, "I'm your biggest fan."

On the way back to the gym, we take the long way around campus and talk. I know that I need to tell her about breaking up with Cindy. "So," I say, "I talked to Cindy this week."

"Oh," Erin says.

"I told her that I thought it was best if we moved on. You know, stayed friends."

"How did she feel about that?" Erin moves closer to me.

"Well, I don't think that she was too excited about it, but I think she understands." I try to make it sound like things went better than they did.

"That must've been hard."

"You know, once it was over, it felt like a giant weight was lifted off my shoulders. I just felt like it wasn't fair to either one of us. She has her life in Cedarville."

"Well, it sounds like you made the right decision, especially if you feel better after talking to her."

Erin and I continue to walk through the campus. The leaves have started to change color, and the smell of fall is in the air. I breathe deep and realize that despite all that has happened with my going to Bertram and leaving all of my best friends, I actually feel happy. I feel an energy that I have never felt before. In Cedarville I was with my best friends, people that I cared about and people who cared about me. But with Erin, at Bertram, it's different. I feel like I can do anything. I try to figure out how I can explain my emotions to Erin without scaring her away.

We complete the loop around campus, and Erin walks me to the front door of the gym. She looks me in the eye and takes my hand into her hand. She smiles her perfect smile and says, "I know breaking it off with Cindy was tough, but I'm glad you did."

"Seriously?"

"Yeah, seriously."

I look at Erin and say, "I'm glad I met you here."

"Me too."

Chapter 21

September 15th

Mr. Tanner opens the cardboard box in front of the room. Some students look on with anticipation, some with dread. No one knows what to expect. The books are black with an orange binding and green writing on the front.

"Mr. Morris, would you help me pass out our new books?" Mr. Tanner asks.

I jump to my feet like it's a football drill. In a short period of time, Mr. Tanner has earned my respect. As I pass out the books, I read the cover: *The Dharma Bums* by: Jack Kerouac. I have heard of Hemingway and Steinbeck, but Kerouac?

"Ladies and gentlemen, raise your hands if you have ever heard of the Beat Generation?" asks Mr. Tanner, smacking the novel into his hand.

No response.

"Allen Ginsberg?"

Nothing. Silence.

"William S. Burroughs?"

Nope.

"*On the Road?*"

Still, no reply.

"Well," Mr. Tanner reflects, "it appears as though I have my work cut out for me. One of my favorite authors of all time is Jack Kerouac. He was a Beatnik. The Beat Generation was characterized by individuals who rebelled against contemporary society. Does anybody here feel that way?"

We all raise our hands.

He continues, "Allen Ginsberg was a famous poet and writer during the fifties. He is best-known for writing his famous poem, *Howl.*" Mr. Tanner pauses for effect and, from memory, begins reciting the first few lines of the poem: *"I saw the best minds of my generation destroyed by the madness."*

He continues, "William S. Burroughs wrote *Naked Lunch* about his heroine addiction. The book was actually banned until court rulings said it could be published. Kerouac's most famous novel is *On the Road*. That novel covered his insane road trips from New York to California and back again with his best friend Dean Moriarty. Kerouac lived the life: living free, hitchhiking, seeing the world, and then writing about it. I think that most of you will find that Kerouac will capture your attention. Zen Buddhism is one of his topics."

The class chuckles and looks at each other.

"Is that funny?" Mr. Tanner asks with a serious expression on his face.

"No," the class replies in unison.

"Good, because by the end of this week we will be meditating like Kerouac and his best friend from the book, Japhy Ryder."

Meditating? Who is this guy? This isn't English class.

"I know what you are all thinking. Meditation?"

I look at Erin, and we nod our heads in agreement.

"Just give it a chance. Kerouac will make you see the world in a different way. We will study the beat writers, and Kerouac's life and his ultimate demise. He was a hero to many."

I don't know how Mr. Tanner does it because when it comes to his class, I actually want to be here.

* * *

As the week passes, I look forward to our meditation day in English class, almost as much as our football game on Friday night.

Mr. Tanner comes into class Friday morning with a blanket and some thin yoga mats. Another student helps him carry them into the room. He proceeds to pass the mats out, and everyone sits down around the room. Tanner explains the lotus position, but he also explains that his bad knees prevent him from achieving that position. Some of the girls in the class demonstrate their flexibility.

"Very good," Mr. Tanner observes. "Now if you can't sit in the lotus position a simple Indian style will do. Just cross your legs like this. Now, take your thumb and pointer finger and touch those two fingers."

Everyone in the class gets into either the lotus position or sits Indian style.

"Now, has anyone ever seen the movie the *Lion King?* Raffiki demonstrated the proper sitting position and hand position."

Everyone's hands shoot up, until we look around realizing that it's a Disney film, and we quickly lower our hands.

"Nothing to be ashamed of," Tanner laughs. "That monkey has a deeper understanding of the world." In his best imitation he says, "Oh, the past can hurt."

The whole class laughs.

"Now, once you are sitting correctly, and your hands are in the right position, we are going to work on breathing, and paying attention to our breath."

The class lets him take us on his little experiment.

"Mr. Morris, how still does Kerouac sit in the pages you read for homework last night?"

I sit up with pride. I haven't missed an assignment since the first day of school. "He sat so still two mosquitoes landed on him and didn't even bite him."

"Mr. Morris, you did the reading. We have a Bodhisattva in class, an enlightened being. Good for you," Mr. Tanner comments with a wink. He continues, "With meditation, you can begin to quiet your mind. You will find a new ability to focus."

Mr. Tanner takes the class through an entire meditation. I sit and breathe and focus on my breath. I try to clear my mind by letting go of all my thoughts. I begin to feel my body relax and my mind clear. I am encouraged by the almost immediate effects. After the meditation, Mr. Tanner starts throwing out information about the Four Noble Truths and the Eight Fold Path. He talks about the fact that all life is suffering, but he tells us that that there is a way to end the suffering. He talks about enlightenment and moments of Satori. By the end of the class, I want to learn all about Zen Buddhism. And as for having a quiet mind, I want that, too.

Mr. Tanner stops class and says, "For those of you who are athletes," he looks over at me, "you might find that meditation can help you with your athletic performance. I am starting a meditation club on Wednesday nights from seven to eight. If you're interested come and see me."

Class ends, and I walk over to Mr. Tanner. "Mr. Tanner, I'd like to be a part of the meditation class."

Tanner puts his hand on my shoulder. "I was hoping you would."

Chapter 22

September 16th

I sit in my dorm reading *The Dharma Bums* when my phone rings.

"Billy, honey, is that you?" My mom's voice comes over the phone.

"Yeah, it's me."

"Oh honey, it's mom. I've been trying to get ahold of you."

"I've been busy," I say.

"Are you okay?" she asks.

"I'm doing fine," I answer shortly.

My mom tries to be friendly. "Listen, I know you're not very happy with me right now, but I want you to know that this decision was not easy."

"Yeah, whatever."

"Billy, I want you to know that I love you. Bertram is a great opportunity for you."

"Mom, I think Bertram was a great opportunity for you to get rid of me. And it looks like things are working out fine . . . for you."

"You know that's not true. There are more opportunities at Bertram than you would ever have back in Cedarville. I believe that with all my heart." She pauses. "How is school going anyway?"

I don't know how to answer her question. If I really think about it, my transfer to Bertram, although very hard at first, has been filled with some positive things: my first varsity football game, Mr. Tanner's English class, and of course Erin.

I begin carefully, "It's been okay, I guess. I have this crazy English teacher who is all wrapped up in Buddhism. I got in a fight with the captain of the football team during practice, and my roommate was taped from head to toe with athletic tape."

My mom is silent. "Well now, that does sound interesting. At least you didn't say you were bored." She laughs on the other end of the line.

My mom always had a way of putting a good spin on things. I had forgotten the times when we were good friends. After my dad moved out, we were actually close. My sister, and my mom and I were brought together by the divorce. We became our own little team, determined to get through the mess.

"Yeah well, I haven't been bored." I can feel my defensive wall crumbling under the kind voice of my mother as I start to understand that her decision to send me to Bertram was one she thought would help me in the long run. For the first time, I believe that she did have my best interest in mind.

"It sounds like you are doing some great things there. Richard and I are planning on coming to Cleveland for Thanksgiving. We will come and spend some time, take you out to dinner."

"Well, I'll be here. I have nowhere else to go."

"It's good to hear your voice. I've been thinking about you and wondering how you were doing. I was about to call the office and tell them I couldn't get ahold of you. I miss you."

"Yeah, it's good to talk to you too."

"You are going to love South Carolina. The weather here is beautiful. It's nice to get out of dreary Dayton. Richard has found a great job, and I have gone on a couple interviews. I may even go back to school. You know I never did get to finish college, having your sister and all. I think it would be kinda fun to be a student again."

"You can take my place," I joke, lightening the mood.

My mom is silent for a moment. "Hey," she says, "let's make Sunday afternoon our talk time. I don't want to go so long without talking to you." She gives me her new number in South Carolina, and we promise to make Sunday our time to talk. Hanging up the phone, I'm glad that I finally talked to my mom.

Chapter 23

September 17th to October 28th

During the next six weeks, our English class studies the Beat Generation, Zen Buddhism, and Jack Kerouac. On that first Wednesday night, I meet a small group of students, including Erin, for a thirty minute meditation led by Mr. Tanner. He keeps me after the meditation class on the first night.

"Mr. Morris, I want to commend you on your attendance tonight and your marked improvement in my class."

I look down at the floor. "I like coming to your class."

Mr. Tanner laughs. "Well, it sounds like a win-win situation. I thought you might be interested in meditation. I think you can benefit a great deal from it."

"I'm interested."

"Do you want to know why I learned meditation?" Tanner asks.

I shrug my shoulders. "Sure."

"When I returned from Vietnam, I was diagnosed with PTSD."

"What's that?" I ask.

"Post Traumatic Stress Disorder. I had bad anxiety attacks. The doctors wanted to put me on all this different medication. I had a friend who was Buddhist, and he suggested I try meditation first. I figured I had nothing to lose. He told me the meditation would help with the anxiety, and he told me the rest of my life would benefit. I couldn't get started soon enough. I was scared to death by the severity of my anxiety. I worked at meditation like my life depended on it, and in a lot of ways, it did."

"How long did it take until you started to feel better?"

"Well, let's just say Vietnam never really goes away, but at least I could handle my life. Meditation can make a difference, but you have to do your part. Would you be interested in enhancing your focus on the football field?"

"I'd like to learn."

Mr. Tanner explains, "You see, there is a thing called mental imagery. It's kind of like seeing plays on the football field before they happen. There's the power of the human mind. More often than not, we predict the outcome of things in our lives before they happen to us."

I look at him and ask, "Mr. Tanner, why are you helping me?"

"Well, Mr. Morris, let's just say I know how it feels to be the new kid."

I want to ask Tanner a million questions, but I simply say, "Thank you."

* * *

We cruise through our football schedule, winning week in and week out. Terrance Strong dominates on the football field. He runs like a machine, and our defense is unstoppable. We end our regular season undefeated, a perfect 9-0. We are ranked 4th in our region for Division IV and psyched for the playoffs.

I make it a point to go to the library study room every night and meditate for thirty minutes on my own. I'm amazed at how much quieter my mind is. I'm able to control my moods and emotions. My ability to focus in class and on the football field improves, and my anticipation is stronger.

But on Saturday after our final game, even though everyone else is celebrating with a pizza party in the cafeteria, I sit alone in my dorm room. I'm a part of the Bertram team, but it doesn't feel like my team. Pulling the newspaper clippings from Cedarville's season out of my desk drawer, I spread them out across my desk. I lean back in my chair and rub my eyes, not sure how I should feel. I wish I was playing with my friends. Looking into the mirror above my desk, I really look at myself, my dark hair, my hazel eyes; I can see that I am no longer a kid. I realize I'm a different person. I'm proud of the person looking back at me from the mirror. Looking down at my desk, I arrange the articles from Cedarville's season, week four to week ten. I read each one:

THE DAYTON FLYER

High School Football: WEEK 4

Cedarville extended its record to a perfect 4-0 by defeating and dominating the Oakwood Hawks by a score of 42-14. Jack Thompson continued to explode on the gridiron. He upped his rushing total to 810 total yards by rushing for 170 yards and 5 touchdowns against a struggling Oakwood team. Cedarville's passing attack was again led by Danny Towers. Towers threw for over 300 yards. Oakwood scored both of their touchdowns late in the fourth quarter. Cedarville hosts Xenia next Friday.

THE DAYTON FLYER

High School Football: WEEK 5

Cedarville stayed undefeated at 5-0 by shutting out Xenia 17-0. Jack Thompson ran for an even 200 yards and one touchdown. Kicker Kevin Humphries added a thirty-five yard field goal at the end of the half to put the Comets up 10-0. Woody Fletcher demonstrated why he's a starting sophomore by adding an interception for a touchdown to clinch the victory for the Comets. Cedarville travels to Columbus Academy next week.

THE DAYTON FLYER

High School Football: WEEK 6

Cedarville stands at 6-0. Columbus Academy boasted about their dynamic duo of tailback and fullback, Chris Snow and Tim Cage, which the Cedarville defense shut down. The running game that was explosive was led by Cedarville's Jack Thompson who ran for 164 yards and 3 touchdowns as the Comets ran away with a 35-17 victory. Danny Towers continued to demonstrate his skills on the football field by throwing for 318 yards and two touchdowns. Chris Snow and Tim Cage were held to 35 yards and 15 yards respectively. Cedarville heads to Westerville next Friday.

THE DAYTON FLYER

High School Football: WEEK 7

Cedarville traveled to Columbus to play a tough Westerville team. Quarterback Danny Towers led the team with 285 yards passing and three touchdowns. Westerville was on the losing end of a 28-21 defeat. Sophomore cornerback Woody Fletcher iced the game when he intercepted a Westerville pass and returned it 70 yards for the game winning touchdown late in the fourth quarter. Jack Thompson kept the Westerville defense honest with 214 yards on 33 carries. Cedarville plays at Middletown next Friday.

THE DAYTON FLYER

High School Football: WEEK 8

Cedarville toppled a tough Middletown team by a score of 14-10. Both touchdowns were scored by a hard-running Jack Thompson. Thompson ran for 245 yards on 35 carries. Cedarville fumbled 4 times inside the Middletown 20 yard line. Coach Murphy attributed the turnovers to the torrential downpour of rain that persisted throughout the night. He was quoted as saying, "That field was a quagmire. I'm surprised there weren't more turnovers by both teams." Cedarville travels to Hamilton next week.

THE DAYTON FLYER

High School Football: WEEK 9

Cedarville defeated Hamilton by a score of 49-7. Quarterback Danny Towers threw for five touchdowns and 325 yards. Hamilton was never in the game. Their only score came with 2 minutes left in the fourth quarter. Jack Thompson added 2 touchdowns and 188 yards on the ground to round out the scoring. Thompson led the defense with 15 tackles and an interception. Cedarville hosts Cincinnati Xavier next Friday night as they attempt to post their first undefeated season.

THE DAYTON FLYER

High School Football: WEEK 10

Cedarville goes a perfect 10-0!!! Jack Thompson has made himself a candidate for Mr. Football in Ohio. In his last regular season game as a sophomore, he ran for 185 yards. That put him over the 2000 yard mark. Cedarville toppled a tough Cincinnati Xavier team by winning 21-7. The humble Thompson was quoted as saying, "This is a team sport. I'm just glad that our team has the opportunity to go to the playoffs." Cedarville will attempt to surpass their semi-final defeat last year by making it to the State Championship Game. This unselfish team will be one to be reckoned with. My only advice to playoff teams is, "Watch out for the Cedarville Comets."

I neatly stack the articles and put them back in my desk drawer. I call Jack, hoping that his dad isn't home.

"Hello," my best friend's voice echoes over the phone. It seems like forever since we last talked.

"Hey, man, it's me," I blurt out.

"Billy? What's up, bro?" Jack asks.

"Not much, just sitting here in my dorm looking over the newspaper articles of your undefeated season. Who would have thought? Jack Thompson, over two thousand yards in just ten games. Dude, you're a monster."

"Yeah man, it's been awesome. Can you believe an undefeated season? Everyone in the town's going nuts. I just want things to be normal. You know, things haven't been normal around here."

"Why? What's up?"

"Well, to start off, Leigh broke up with me. She says I'm out of control."

"Really?"

"Yeah, can you believe it? And to make matter worse, my dad got his second DUI this week."

"I thought he lost his license?"

"Yeah, that's just it. He got another one on a suspended license. The police made him do the sobriety test, walk the line, and say the alphabet. To top it off, it was after a game. The football bus passed my old man walking the line. All the seniors started busting on me, telling me my old man's a drunk. I flew out of my seat and punched Tolliger right in the mouth. The whole back of the bus broke out into a brawl. Coach Murphy had the driver pull over, and he made the whole team jog the back roads all the way to school."

"Man, I bet Murphy was pissed."

"Man, I thought his head was going to explode. His face turned this dark shade of purple. We knew we were in trouble."

"Did everybody make it back to school?"

"Yeah, we made it," Jack says.

"I've been reading about you guys. It sounds like you've been tearing up the league."

"I don't know man. Football is my only outlet. My dad's driving me crazy. He comes home drunk, pissed off. Thursday night is dollar beer night at the Tavern. He comes home all liquored up and starts pushing me around, telling me how worthless I am. He usually throws a couple a punches until he passes out. So when it comes game time, I got this anger inside me, and I have to get it out. It's like somebody turns a switch. I put that helmet on, and it's revenge time. Whoever we're playing, they pay for every punch and every insult my dad throws at me. Every time he tells me I'm nothing, stupid, weak, I feel like I'm going to fly into a rage. By the time Friday night rolls around, I don't even want to just play the other team. I want to kill 'em, make 'em pay. It's like I'm some possessed animal. I hit this one kid so hard, I broke his jaw, knocked some of his teeth out."

Jack sounds like a different person. With his mother gone, he really has nowhere to turn. I ask him, "What can I do to help?"

"You can get me the hell out of here before I snap. My old man has to go to court. He may have to go to jail. I don't know what I'm going to do. Right now he's out on bail and guess where he is?"

"The Tavern?"

"You got it," Jack says, sounding defeated.

"What are you going to do?"

"I don't know. It's tough. You know, pressure from the coaches, my old man, it's starting to wear on me. We have our first playoff game this Friday. The only thing that's getting me through this is football." He pauses. "And you. I feel better when I can talk to you and get some of this stuff off my chest."

"What about your mom?" I ask.

"Haven't heard from her."

"What does Coach Murphy have to say about all this?"

"He said he would help if I needed anything."

"What can I do?" I ask.

"Just be a friend."

Chapter 24

October 30th

Mr. Tanner strolls into class with new boxes filled with our next novel. He calls for my assistance in passing out the books. I jump from my seat. As I pass them out, I check out the cover. The novel is blue with a drawing of an armadillo on the cover. The title reads, *A Prayer for Owen Meany*, by John Irving. I wonder what could be better than Jack Kerouac. The book is more than 500 pages. At Cedarville I had never even read a novel, let alone one this big!

Mr. Tanner pulls me aside and quietly says, "Once you get started, you won't be able to put it down."

Mr. Tanner addresses the class once all the books have been handed out. "Our newest author is John Irving. He has written some classic novels: The *Cider House Rules*, *The World According to Garp*, and *A Widow for One Year*. I think that you will find *A Prayer for Owen Meany* to be very enjoyable."

We read the first chapter aloud. It's titled "The Foul Ball." The chapter is completely confusing, and I wonder how I am going to get through the book.

Mr. Tanner says, "For those of you that are a bit confused, don't lose heart. I'll go over the readings in detail. Once you get it, the story really flows. Plus it deals with some weighty issues: religion, best friends, and the death of loved ones, both the good and difficult things that life tends to throw at us and asks us to figure out."

I feel like Mr. Tanner is a mind reader, like he is talking directly to me. I decide to give Mr. Tanner and the novel my best effort.

After class, I meet Erin in the hall. "How are you doing?" I ask.

"Great," she says, as she smiles that perfect smile. She pushes me on the shoulder. "Are you looking forward to the game this Friday?"

"Yeah, but I'm nervous. It's hard to believe that the playoffs are already here. Everybody acts like it's no big deal."

"Well, everybody's really excited. The whole school is buzzing."

"Do you want to meet for lunch?" I suggest. "I need to talk to Mr. Tanner before my next class."

Erin playfully pushes my shoulder. "I'll see you at lunch."

I walk up the stairs to Mr. Tanner's office. He's sitting at his desk reading Herman Melville's *Moby Dick*. I knock, and he glances up and says, "Ah, Mr. Morris, do come in. What can I do for you?"

I don't know where to start, but it all just comes out, the whole story. I tell him about Cedarville, my mom and Dick moving, Jack and his old man, Cindy, Erin, football.

Surprisingly, Mr. Tanner doesn't flinch. "Being a kid ain't easy," he says. "And, I have some news for you. Life . . . it isn't easy, and the sooner you figure that out, the better. All you can do is make the best of what you got. And from here, it seems like you got a lot going for you. You're a strong athletic kid, and you have a pretty good head on your shoulders. And from what I can tell, the best part about you is that you can be this tough-guy-football-player, but you have this whole other side of you that is about caring and compassion. And that might be your best quality."

I've never had anyone mention anything to me about my compassion.

"You know," he adds, "the thing I learned from Vietnam is that everything is temporary, even the bad stuff. The way I look at it is you don't have it so bad. You're at one of the best prep schools in the state, your football team is undefeated, and you're playing in your first playoff game this Friday night. From where I'm sitting, things could be a whole lot worse."

I agree with Mr. Tanner, but my worry and focus has shifted from my own problems to Jack's. I explain, "I feel helpless, like there's nothing I can do to help him. And the worst part of all of this is I'm not there."

"Your buddy Jack sounds pretty tough, cut from the same mold as you I imagine. I have a feeling he's going to be alright. The only things you can do now are the things that you are doing. Keep in touch with him. Let him know you are there for him. Let him know that you are his friend. I'm sure when you talk to him you feel the same way."

It feels good to talk to Mr. Tanner, someone who understands things. He's not just a great teacher; he's a great friend.

I get up from the chair in Mr. Tanner's office and shake his hand. "Thanks for talking."

"Anytime," he nods, "my door is always open."

A thick blanket of snow shrouds Bertram Academy. It collects high on the bare branches, and there's a welcome silence that pervades the campus. The wind blows as I trudge to the cafeteria to meet Erin. I contemplate the advice that Mr. Tanner gave me. He's right. Things could be a whole lot worse. I promise myself to do everything in my power to help Jack, and I pray that he'll be okay.

Chapter 25

October 31st to November 2nd

The week before our first playoff game seems to drag, which makes my anxiety unbearable. For once, I'm glad to have school to occupy my thoughts. All the students talk about the big game in the hallways, in classes, and at lunch. I can't escape "the game."

At practice, it's business as usual. The seniors don't seem as nervous as I am. Terrance Strong is as cool as the come; nothing bothers him, especially since he's signing his letter of intent to play college football. He has been the recruiting target of every major college: The Ohio State Buckeyes, Michigan, Penn State, Florida State, Miami, and Notre Dame. He takes it all in stride. During the season, Terrance got letters and phone calls from Joe Paterno and Bobby Bowden. He's a celebrity at age 17.

After practice on Tuesday, Terrance sees me in the locker room. "Hey Morris, what's up?"

"Not much," I reply splashing some water on my face. "Just a little nervous for the game."

"Yeah, I know, I felt the same way my sophomore year." Terrance fixes his hair in the mirror. "Everything seemed so new, but once you put that helmet on, get on that field, all that melts away. You're in the zone; nothing's going to bother you there."

I have to agree. Once the game starts and that helmet is on, there is nothing that I can't do. I make a complete transformation. Talking to Terrance about the game makes me feel a lot better.

"Hey, what are you going to do about schools? Have you decided?" Immediately I feel like I've crossed the line into his business.

Terrance glances over at me. "Yeah, I think I made up my mind. It's been a tough decision you know. Lots of people making lots of promises." He pauses and looks at me through my reflection in the mirror. "Why? What do you think? Where do you think I should go? What would you do?"

Was Terrance asking my opinion? "Well," I begin cautiously, "I would have to say Penn State. Joe seems like a stand up guy. You know the importance of education and everything. It seems like he really cares about his players. He makes sure they graduate."

Terrance smiles, but he doesn't give away the secret. He will save that for Thursday evening when he signs his letter of intent.

* * *

Thursday night, Terrance is dressed up like he's going to meet the president or something: a maroon three-piece-suit, tie, shined black leather shoes, and a corsage his mother gave him.

At the press conference, he presents his mom a single red rose in front of the team, most of the student body at Bertram, and just about every newspaper reporter in Cleveland.

Terrance sits at a long table in the library and talks into the microphone. "I just want to thank some people. First, I have to thank my mom." He looks over at her and nods his head. "I want to thank my coaches and my teammates. They made this all possible."

He thanks just about everybody on the planet.

He reads his comments from a sheet of paper. "This decision has been the hardest one in my life. I want to thank everyone for their support." When he gets to the bottom of the page, he looks out over the crowd and takes a deep breath. "I will be playing football at Penn State University." Everybody claps. He stands up and hugs his mother who looks like the proudest woman in the world. Like a pro already, he heads over to the reporters and begins to answer questions.

Chapter 26

November 7th

I am freaking out. We board the school bus and begin a half hour ride to what the state calls a mutual site. The bus is quiet; everyone knows the gravity of our first playoff game. I sit next to Sean and slide on my headphones. I listen to my *Rocky* mix, a little *Eye of the Tiger* and all the best songs from each movie. I think about Jack and Cedarville. He too will play in his first playoff game tonight. I talked to Jack after Terrance's announcement, and I told him what a huge production it was. Jack couldn't believe it. He said that maybe one day we could have a press conference and tell everybody where we wanted to go to school to play ball.

On the bus ride, I think about all the hype that comes with a first playoff game. All the reporters, photographers, and cameramen are at our school during practice interviewing the coaches and some of the players. Coach Carlson is constantly warning us about getting caught up in the "perfume" as he likes to call it, people telling you how great you are, and how sometimes you start to believe them. He explains it like this, "A little perfume, it smells nice, but if you drink the perfume, bad stuff happens."

I read a newspaper article about the team we are playing. Springfield is a town like Cedarville, just west of Columbus. The article described how all the players are best friends, how they couldn't wait for the opportunity to be seniors and play in the state playoffs. Coach Carlson, who I'm sure watched hours of film on Springfield, was quoted in the paper. "They are a great team with lots of good players at the skill positions. Their quarterback is a jitterbug with a gun for an arm."

The words stick in my head. How do we catch a jitterbug, and how do we stop a quarterback with a gun for an arm? And more importantly, does our team share the same kind of comradery that Springfield has? All those kids grew up together, they are probably great friends. They want to win, not just for themselves, for each other.

The breaks on the bus squeal and the doors swing open. Coach Carlson stands up and everyone is silent. "This is it guys. Let's get focused and pull it together. Let's get it going!"

Everybody files off the bus, grabs their shoulder pads and helmets from the equipment van, and heads to the locker room. The mood is somber, quiet. Something is missing; there is a lack of energy. Maybe the playoffs are old hat for seniors, but not for me. I can barely keep myself together.

Coach Carlson calls the team together and gives his pep talk. But I can't pay attention. I can't concentrate on what he's saying. It just looks like his mouth is moving. We say the "Our Father" and move out to the field. The locker rooms are 200 yards away from the field.

I hear the band playing and drums pounding, like some ancient Native American ritual. The stands are dotted with gray and mostly red sweatshirts on the Bertram side. The pep bus brought students from the Bertram campus. The other side of the bleachers is filled with the entire Springfield community. I imagine the empty town of Springfield. Their bleachers are a sea of purple and black, and the fans pour out onto the track that surrounds the field. They carry signs that read: PURPLE PEOPLE EATERS. My heart pounds as we walk through the gates and over the track. I slide on my helmet and snap on my chinstrap. I'm ready for battle.

The Springfield team wears black jerseys with purple pants and numbers. They all have mullets hanging out of the back of their helmets. These kids are good old farm boys, sloppy strong. And after the kickoff and my first contact of the game, I learn that they love to hit.

Maybe because Bertram won the State Championship last year, everyone assumes that the competition will lie down, but it's just the opposite. Springfield is out for blood. And for the first time all season, we are losing to the PURPLE PEOPLE EATERS at halftime 13 to 3. We're in a dogfight.

Terrance Strong speaks up at halftime before the coaches get into the locker room. "EVERYBODY WAKE UP!" He moves around the locker room, getting into everyone's face. WHAT ARE WE DOING OUT THERE?" He slams his helmet against a locker. "WE GOT ONE HALF TO MAKE THIS RIGHT, OR OUR SEASON IS OVER. IS THAT WHAT YOU WANT? IS THIS WHAT YOU WANT?" He's completely fired up. "LET'S GO! WE AIN'T DONE YET!"

As Terrance finishes his rant, the coaches move into the locker room in a much calmer fashion. They break the team up into position meetings, trying to get everybody together, trying to figure out how to win the game. They draw X's and O's on the chalkboards, and they ask us why certain plays aren't working. Everything the coaches do at halftime makes a difference, but it is Terrance's words that wake us up.

With a feeling of desperation, we charge the field for the second half. I think Springfield is surprised when the third quarter starts. The hitting, which was ferocious in the first half, elevates to an even greater intensity. On a sweep play, Marcus and I meet their tailback head-on. We drive through him and force him out of bounds. I can hear the running back groan as we crush him into the ground. Everyone on the sideline cheers and congratulates us. We jump to our feet, give each other high fives, and sprint back to the huddle, ready for more.

In the second half, bodies are flying everywhere. It's nasty, intense, and I love it. My nervousness subsides, and I feel like my focus is back. I use what I learned from Mr. Tanner about meditation, and calm myself down. I'm in the zone.

Terrance takes some of his own advice and puts on a running display in the third quarter. Unfortunately, two turnovers, a fumble and an interception keep the score:

Springfield 13 Bertram 3.

In the fourth quarter, Terrance breaks one open. Springfield has contained him for three full quarters, but he breaks some long runs in the fourth. On a sweep to the right, he explodes through a tackle and slips around the right end. He's off to the races. His shoulders swing from side to side as he runs for a fifty-two yard touchdown. The Bertram fans go crazy. The score is 13-9. Our kicker comes in for the extra point. The snap is fumbled by the holder Mike Giffin, who tries to position the ball. He doesn't get the ball set in time, and our kicker boots it way left. We are down by five with only five minutes to go in the game.

Coach Kaplan pulls the defense together and screams with his hoarse voice, "We need the ball back, fast. This is it, guys. You must play as much with your head as your heart. Don't quit. Don't give up. We can win the game."

We sprint out to their thirty-five yard line and huddle up. On the first play, Springfield runs a dive play to their tailback over the right tackle. Sean slants right into the play and puts a solid hit on their tailback, just as he is getting the handoff from the quarterback. Marcus hits the ball carrier at the same time, as he blitzes from his linebacker position. He rips the ball free, and Sean jumps on the fumble. We have the ball back with just less than five minutes in the game deep in their territory.

Terrance is a marked man. Springfield knows he's going to get the ball. The question is whether or not they can stop him. On the first play, Terrance runs another sweep to the wide side of the field. He tries to get to the corner, but their corner back has been playing solid all night. He comes up and wraps up Terrance. I hear the Bertram fans groan, and I feel victory slipping from our hands. Coach Carlson tries a fullback trap on the next play. Sammy Jones never gets a good handle on it, and the ball comes loose. There is a mad scramble for the ball. Bodies fly everywhere, trying to recover the fumble. Somehow, Mike Giffin recovers the ball under a heap of bodies.

Coach Carlson calls a time out after he recovers from his near heart attack. He brings the team together and tries to calm us down as he explains the importance of executing the next play.

"Listen," he begins, "the ball is on the left hash. Terrance's touchdown at the beginning of the fourth quarter was around the right end. That corner will not let that happen again. He'll run up like gangbusters. We must the run. We must sell the run." With that everyone knows where he's going. "We're gonna run the half back pass. That corner will bite, and hopefully so will the safety." He looks at our wide receiver, Willy Davis. "Willy, block your man for a count of three, then slide off him and get your butt in the end zone. Men, this is your time. This is your game. Make it happen."

The offense breaks the huddle and sprints onto the field. The stadium that was rocking with noise becomes strangely quiet. The play moves in slow motion as Mike Giffin takes the snap and pitches the ball wide to Terrance. Standing on the sideline, I see the corner read the sweep. He gets off Willy's block and breaks toward Terrance. When Terrance brings the ball up like he is going to throw, the cornerback's eyes widen. He, and the safety, committed too soon. Willy is wide open in the end zone. All Terrance has to do is get the ball to him. Terrance reaches back and lets the ball go. It wobbles end over end. The backside safety sprints toward Willy, but Willy is so wide open, even though the pass is a duck, he still catches it. Touchdown!! The crowd goes wild, and it takes me out of my trance. We are up 15 to 13. Coach Carlson decides to go for two. Mike pitches the ball out to Terrance, and this time he keeps it, slipping into the end zone to make the score 17 to 13. There are still three minutes left in the game.

We kick off deep to their ten yard line. Their wide receiver breaks a tackle and returns the ball to the forty-five yard line. There is 2:04 left on the clock. Marcus calls a man-to-man defense, which we rarely play. The man-to-man defense has me locked on their tight end. On their first play from scrimmage, they fake a hand off to their tailback. I bite on the fake, and my man, the tight end, runs wide open across the field. The jitterbug with a gun for an arm, hits him with a pass in perfect stride. I sprint down the sideline. I start to close the gap as their tight end nears the end zone. Somehow, forty-five yards later, I literally jump onto his back around the twelve yard line and drive him into the ground on our seven yard line. All I can think is that my mistake just cost us the game.

Terrance comes over to me and shouts, "IT'S OVER. IT'S OVER. CAN'T LET THAT PLAY RUIN THE NEXT ONE. KEEP YOUR HEAD UP. WE NEED YOU."

There is still 1:45 left in the game. It is their ball—first and goal. On the first play, they run a sweep to the right. Their linemen pull to the right in perfect unison. They drive and cut block our defensive linemen, but that frees up Marcus. He shoots through the line like a bolt of lightning and takes down the running back, making the stop.

On second down, the quarterback takes a fast three-step drop and throws a quick slant pass. The ball is low, and the receiver dives for it. The ball skips off the grass into the arms of the Springfield receiver who is on the ground, but the referee, who is blocked by all the bodies, calls it complete. The entire defense jumps in the referee's face pleading our case.

"Incomplete! Incomplete!" I shout. "That wasn't even close. You couldn't even see that play."

The referee looks at me. "Son," he shouts over the boos from the crowd, "watch yourself, or you'll be out of the game."

Marcus grabs me by the shoulder pads and pulls me back toward the huddle. "Don't be stupid, man! Keep your head about you."

I walk backward to the huddle facing the referee, who I can see is just waiting for me to say one more thing.

It's third down and goal from the three yard line. Their quarterback drops back and throws a fade to the corner of the end zone. The wide receiver makes a great inside move on our corner, like the slant route, and our corner back bites on the fake. The receiver breaks back outside to the corner of the end zone. He's wide open. The quarterback pauses, seeing his receiver so wide open; he wants to make the perfect pass. He pulls back and floats the ball toward the corner of the end zone. Just as the ball is about to land in the receiver's outstretched hands, Terrance, from his safety position, knocks the ball to the ground. The quarterback's moment of hesitation costs him the completion. We sprint over to Terrance and give him high fives. He's more relieved than excited.

Their coach calls time out. It's fourth down. Coach Kaplan jogs out onto the field with his headset around his neck. He comes into the defensive huddle. He is somehow calm. "Last play guys. Step up. You can do this. Even though they're on the three yard line, they may try to throw. Their quarterback is their best player. I wouldn't be surprised if they put the game in his hands. LET'S GO!" He jogs back to the sideline. Marcus calls the defense, a regular 52 with man-to-man coverage on the receivers. I will not be fooled again.

The referee blows the whistle, and Springfield hustles to the line of scrimmage. Marcus and I call out the defensive signals. "Lion, Lion, Stick 44, Lion."

Their quarterback calls the signals, "Black 18, Black 18, set, hut, hut." He takes the snap and rolls out to his right.

Coach Kaplan guessed right. They put the game in the hands of their best player. He scrambles back and forth, and I mirror him from my linebacker position, and slowly drift into the end zone, keeping my man in my sight. He hooks in behind me and sits in the back of the end zone. Suddenly, everything stops. My eyes meet the eyes of their quarterback. He releases the ball, a perfect spiral; only it comes in my direction. I step to my right and intercept the ball six yards deep in our own end zone.

My first reaction is complete surprise; my second is to run like hell. I sprint toward the left sideline. Their receiver runs at me full speed from the corner of the end zone. But I don't see their quarterback who takes a direct course at my right knee. He dives in toward the ligaments in my knee, hoping to get me back for the interception. He chops my knees out from under me. Still in slow motion, I describe a complete circle in the air and land hard.

When I jump to my feet, real time resumes, and I'm smothered by the entire defense. They shout, "Way to go, man! You did it!"

The parents and students go crazy in the stands. We win the game, and I'm the hero. The celebration begins.

Chapter 27

November 8th

I'm dying to know how Cedarville did in their first playoff game. I tried calling Jack on his cell last night, but all I got was his voicemail. When I get to the library, I hold my breath as I spread the paper out on the table and scan the sports page and read about Cedarville's first playoff game:

THE DAYTON FLYER

High School Football

The Cedarville Comets started their playoff odyssey against the West Jefferson Blue Knights last night. The Comets came out throwing the ball using their powerful tailback, Jack Thompson, as a decoy. Quarterback Danny Towers threw all over the West Jefferson defense. His accurate passes punctured the Knight's defense. After establishing a 28 point half time lead, the ball was given to Thompson, who punished the Jefferson defenders. He had 28 carries for 120 yards. Most of his yards and his only touchdown came in the second half. The Cedarville defense was led by sophomore Woody Fletcher who had two interceptions. West Jefferson's Lionel Smith scored one touchdown late in the fourth quarter. Cedarville won 35-7. They will face Cincinnati Wyoming next Friday night at Dayton's Welcome Stadium.

I look up from the newspaper, and Erin is standing directly in front of me, her usual Saturday morning attire, sweat pants and baseball hat. There's something about her eyes, their comfort, and their acceptance.

"I knew you'd be here," she says, sitting down next to me.

"Yeah, I had to check up on Cedarville."

Erin studies my face. "So . . . what was the score?"

"Thirty-five to seven, they won. Their quarterback threw for three touchdowns."

Erin looks like she's impressed. "How did your friend Jack do?"

"120 yards rushing and a touchdown."

"Wow, not a bad night."

"Yep," I say, feeling kind of empty inside.

"So then what's the matter? Why do you look so down?" Erin asks.

I shake my head. "It's nothing."

"After your game last night, I figured you'd be excited."

"I guess it's cool and all playing in the playoffs with *the* Terrance Strong, but it's not the same. Playing for Cedarville was different. The guys here are good guys, but it's not even close to playing with the friends you grew up with. I want to be playing with them."

"I know you're frustrated, but did you hear the Bertram fans last night? After you made that interception, everyone was yelling, 'Who was that? Where did that kid come from?' It was awesome. You were the man; you were the hero. I was so excited for you, and not because of the interception. I was proud of you because all I could think about were the things you've overcome to get to this point, to make that kind of difference in so many peoples' lives."

Erin really makes me think. I have had to prove myself over and over, and I've had to do it away from my friends and my family. "Thanks a lot," I say.

Erin gets this look like she's considering an important question. "You can thank me by coming to the school play."

"I wouldn't miss it. When is it?" I ask.

"Thursday night," Erin says with a hope-filled look.

I give her the thumbs up. "It's a deal."

"It's Shakespeare, but it's a comedy. I think you might like it," Erin tries to convince me, even though she doesn't need to.

"If you're in it, I can't see why I wouldn't."

"It's about love at first sight, then there's some confusion, but it all works out in the end."

"Sounds like my life," I mumble under my breath.

"What?" Erin asks.

"Nothing." I look around the library, making sure the coast is clear. I lean toward her and put my hands on her lower back, touching her skin. She leans into me, and her fingers rub the back of my neck. She pulls me to her, and we kiss for a long minute. The kiss is everything I thought it would be. I don't want to let her go. Eventually, we separate and kind of look at each other, at a loss for words.

Erin finally says, "Wow. That was really . . . nice."

I just nod my head because I can't find the words. Things feel awkward.

"So, I, um, I have play practice tonight. So I guess I'll see you tomorrow."

"Okay," I say, barely able to speak.

Erin gives me a hug, and I kiss her again. I can't even begin to describe the feeling. It's like everything in the world makes sense.

She walks out of the library, and I can't even get up. On the chair at the far end of the library, I start to think. Three months ago, I thought my life was over and that I was going to lose touch with all of my friends. I was more afraid than I thought I ever could be. Since then, I made a game-saving interception, and I met the coolest girl ever. But I was torn between two worlds: Bertram and Cedarville.

I can't get the image out of my mind: my best friends playing together and me not being there. I reread the article from the Cedarville game. I imagine Jack punishing the defenders on the other team, them trying to take him down, and Jack, dragging them into the end zone. I picture myself in my Bertram uniform, and it just doesn't feel right. And even though I feel this awesome connection with Erin, part of me feels like things are not the way they're supposed to be. Talk about being completely confused.

* * *

On Sunday night I get a call from my mother. "Hello," I answer.

"Hi, honey. How have you been?" she asks.

How can I explain to her that I made a game-saving interception, met the girl of my dreams, and found an English teacher that has changed my life? How can I explain to her that I don't know how I feel, how I miss my friends back in Cedarville? Where should I start? I say, "Things here are . . . different."

"Different is good, I guess," my mom chuckles. "Hey, I really miss you, and I've been thinking a lot about you. I've been reading the paper and following your football season. Both Bertram and Cedarville are undefeated. That's pretty exciting. I can't believe there's a chance that you might play each other. Richard and I are planning to come to Cleveland for Thanksgiving and the week after. We could come for a game. I would love to see you."

"Yeah, I guess that would be fine," I answer. Part of me is excited to see my mom, and the other part is still angry at her. I resent that she left me on Bertram's doorstep, and now after all my hard work, she is just going to show up. I don't think it's fair. I don't feel like she deserves to be a part of it. Plus, I dread the thought of Dick giving me pointers on how to play the game.

"Well, that settles it. We will make our way up around Thanksgiving. We'll get to see you play."

"Yeah, if we make it that far," I respond half-heartedly.

"Oh, don't be silly. Of course you guys are going to make it. By the way," my mother redirects the conversations, "have you talked to Cindy?"

It seems like forever since I thought about Cindy. Four months ago, we talked about staying together after high school. Now after coming to Bertram and meeting Erin, my world has been turned upside down. I'm not sure where to begin. I tell her, "I haven't really talked to Cindy. We kinda lost touch."

"Well, don't lose heart," my mom says. "I'm sure there are plenty of girls there that are probably just too shy to talk to the star of the football team."

"I'm not the star of the team, mom."

"That's not what I've been reading in the newspaper."

"How did you get Cleveland's newspaper down in South Carolina?" I ask.

"Oh, it's on the school's website. They keep it pretty well updated, especially with the team in the playoffs."

"How did you know about Cedarville?" I ask suspiciously.

"A friend from back home has been sending me clippings of all the games from the newspaper."

"What friend?" I ask.

"Just an old friend from the Paper Factory." My mother sounds reluctant to give me any more details. "Billy, I want you to know that I love you. I've been thinking about you every day. Good luck in your game this week. We'll be there soon. I can't wait to see you."

"I'll see you soon," I say.

I hang up and stare out the window and think about playing Cedarville in the State Championship game. My heart skips a beat. My whole life I anticipated playing on the same team with all of my friends, and now there was a chance that just the opposite could happen. I might face my best friends on the biggest stage in high school sports. I wanted to play football with my friends, but I didn't want it this way.

Chapter 28

November 9th

It's early Monday morning, and Mr. Tanner does it again. He gets me thinking when he says, "Faith and doubt often collide when it comes to religion, especially when there's no hard core evidence that a God exists."

No one knows what to say.

I pull out *A Prayer for Owen Meany*, and I run my finger over the cover, curious to find out what happens next. Funny enough, I really do want to know.

Mr. Tanner looks around the room as students flip through the pages of the book. "Fate, destiny, it's been around for as long as humans have been around. It's been in literature since Beowulf. We'll talk about Beowulf and Grendel later," he says, as he smiles, knowing what awaits us. "I love this book for one simple reason. It's about the roles that we play in other people's lives. We have the ability to influence people in such profound ways, life-changing ways. In this way, we are all instruments of God. Every thing we do and say, no matter how big or small, affects the people that we meet on a daily basis. If our intentions are good, we all can make a positive difference in the world. Ralph Waldo Emerson once said that success is about making peoples' lives better. Sometimes we can do that by being a good friend, helping someone in need, or sometimes it's as simple as a phone call." He glances in my direction.

We begin reading chapter two out loud. It's slow at first, too much background. Mr. Tanner promises that the action will pick up, and the book will be worthwhile. At the end of the class, we are about fifteen pages into the chapter. He closes his book and sets it down on the desk that he sits on. He rocks forward on his hands and says, "This is one of my favorite novels. It has great characters. It's hilarious, but most importantly, it's about friendship, the sacrifices friends make for each other. I may go so far as to say that true friendship, a really good friend, could be the most important thing in the world."

Jack Thompson, of all my Cedarville friends, he was the one who made sure to call. He was the one who made me feel better when my mother decided to send me to Bertram. He was the one who, despite everything he was dealing with at home, made a point to make sure I was okay.

* * *

On Thursday night, I'm relieved to have my mind on something other than the game. I put on a pair of corduroy pants, a powder blue button down shirt, and my barn jacket to walk across the already dark campus. On my way to see my first play, I hear the buzz of the iron street lamps that line the walkway from the dorms to the auditorium. The newly shoveled sidewalk glistens. The salt crunches under my shoes. I look out onto the woods that surround the campus. The snowflakes fall softly in front of the lights, and each branch supports the weight of the snow. It's a silence I never knew in Cedarville.

I enter the auditorium and sit in the back row. I read the program: The Bertram Academy Theater Presents: William Shakespeare's: *Much Ado about Nothing*. The auditorium lights go down as the stage lights go up. When the play starts, a man runs into the center of the stage announcing that a bunch of people are returning from battle. He throws out names like Don Pedro, Claudio, Benedick, and Don John. I'm confused by the beginning of the play, but none of that matters when the next scene begins and Erin has her first big part. She is one of the lead actresses, Hero, the daughter of the town's Governor. That part, I understand.

Erin reinvents herself in so many ways: musician, singer, actress, and athlete. And it is then that it hits me, Mr. Tanner's words about friendship and fate. Erin came into my life and affected me like no one else ever has. She is talented and smart, but above and beyond that she is a friend, a great friend.

So here I am in the auditorium, and unbelievably, liking Shakespeare. I'm laughing and smiling, enjoying Erin's performance. She brings her character to life. When the play ends, all of the actors stand at the front of the stage to take a bow. The audience claps wildly, and Erin smiles her All-American smile. All I can think is that I found the most amazing girl.

I meet Erin after the play and say, "Hey, great job tonight. I'm really proud of you." Saying nice things is something that Erin has taught me. I was never good at communicating things like that, but she does it so freely. I've learned that showing you are proud of someone and telling them is really important.

"Thanks for coming. I'm glad you made it." She gives me a big hug and introduces me to the other cast members. I recognize some of them from around school and in my classes, but I have never really met them. It's cool to meet a whole new group of people. There's a pizza party after the play with all of the actors and stagehands. I actually meet a couple of pretty nice people. Jack would get a kick out of this—me hanging out with a bunch of actors.

In the middle of the party, Erin walks over to me while I am talking to my newest acting friend and says, "C'mon, let's get out of here."

Walking out the door of the auditorium I ask Erin, "Can I walk you home?"

"I was kinda hoping you would." There is a chatter of voices from the people on the snowy walkway. Erin asks, "So what did you think?"

I reach for her hand. "Honestly, I didn't think I was going to like it, but it was really, really good. You were awesome. It was funny, too. I never thought in a million years that I would like a play, especially Shakespeare, but maybe I just liked it because you were in it."

"You're too sweet." Erin looks right at me.

"I actually laughed out loud. Dogberry and Verges were hilarious. I always thought Shakespeare was dark and violent, you know death and insanity and all that."

"He wrote some dark stuff, but he also wrote great comedies. I love the part where Claudio and Don Pedro are tricked by Don John."

"That scene was great. Those actors actually became those other people."

"They all want to be professional actors. They take it very seriously. It's their passion, kinda like how you play football. Bertram has an excellent drama department. Maybe you should try out for the spring play?"

"Who, me? No way. I would embarrass myself. I'll stick to running track."

"Suit yourself, but I think you'd be fantastic."

I want the walk to last forever, but we soon arrive at her dorm. Erin turns and looks at me and says, "Do you want to come in for a minute? My roommate went home for the weekend." My knees get weak, and my heart starts racing, or it stops, I can't tell which. She leans into me and kisses me on the cheek. "Come on in. Curfew isn't for another forty-five minutes."

"Yeah, okay." I follow her to her second floor room. She opens the door and turns on the light. Her room is a lot neater than mine. It actually smells good, too. She moves across the room and turns on her CD player. The song is *Sugar Mountain*. She explains who Neil Young is, how he was her dad's favorite singer while she was growing up, how it makes her feel safe. I listen to the music, and I am hooked. The strum of the guitar and cry of the harmonica put me on Sugar Mountain, wherever it is. I look at Erin, and I know I am in love.

She walks over to her bed and sits down. She pats the area next to her suggesting that I come and sit down. I point to the bed and then to myself. She shakes her head and rolls her eyes.

I walk slowly over to her bed and sit down beside her. Almost in the same motion, she leans over and kisses my lips. Her tongue lightly caresses my tongue, and we kiss, kiss like I have never kissed before. It's tender, passionate. I bring her close to me and hold her. We fall back onto the pillows and look into each other's eyes and laugh.

"I've wanted to do that since the first day I saw you," she says.

"Me, too," I agree.

We listen to the rest of the CD; each song gets ingrained in my mind. On this night, my heart is open, completely vulnerable. The possibility of sex crosses my mind, but it occurs to me that just being there, holding Erin in my arms is the best thing in the world.

"Do you want to know why I came to Bertram?" she asks.

"Sure, if you want to tell me."

"My mom and dad got divorced last year, and my mom had a really tough time. She kind of had like a nervous breakdown. After my dad left, I guess she couldn't handle it. We didn't have a lot of money, so my mom applied for the scholarships at Bertram."

"You seem to be dealing pretty well with all that. You sure don't let it show."

"I guess that's why I like my music and acting so much. It's my way to escape. I put all my emotions in those things. When I'm on that stage, playing that violin, or acting out another person's life, I don't have to think about all the things in my life. I love playing the violin. I get lost in the music. I go to a different place."

"I know what you mean. It's like football for me. When I put on that helmet, I know there is nothing that can hurt me. It's the only place where I feel like I have control. It's like it's my world. You know it's weird, I guess everybody's got something in their life. Nobody's got it easy."

"It's horrible, isn't it?" Erin says.

"Horrible . . . and great. Since I've come to Bertram, I've changed a lot, and I'm starting to like who I am. I like how I came here and earned a position on this team, how I told myself that nothing was going to keep me down. I think the bad stuff, the hard stuff, makes you better, stronger."

"Yeah, I guess I never really looked at it that way," Erin says.

"I've really changed a lot."

Erin looks around her room. "You know, when I first met you, I thought you were this typical jock."

"Yeah, so what changed?"

Erin shrugs her shoulders. "I don't know. It's just something about you. You're not like the rest. When I look in your eyes, I don't see that kind of person. I see something different. I see someone who cares about people, his friends, his team. I see someone who cares about me."

"You've helped me a lot since I got here."

"You've done the same for me." Erin holds my hand.

"I mean, coming to my games and helping me with school."

"What about you? Coming to my recitals, my games, and the play," she says.

"I wouldn't have missed it for the world."

Erin looks over at her clock. "I hate to say it, but it's getting close to curfew. You better go."

She walks me to the door and before she opens it, she kisses me on the lips. Her hand caresses the back of my neck, and my whole body tingles.

I lean into her body and can feel her against me. Reluctantly, I let go and move toward the door.

"I'll see you tomorrow," she says, as she closes the door behind me. On the way to my dorm under the large snowflakes, I breathe in the crisp winter air.

Chapter 29

November 14th

The snow comes down and sticks to the turf. The school maintenance crew from Baldwin-Wallace College shovels the snow off the white paint that lines the field. The stadium is filled to capacity for the state semi-final playoff game.

I jog on the field and look around. Our stands are blanketed with our team colors: red, black and gray. The other side of the stands is filled with the green and white of the Archbold Pirates. Terrance slaps me on the shoulder pads. "Let's get going, Morris."

Coach Kaplan huddles the defense and begins, "Keep focused on the game." The roar of the crowd forces him to shout his instructions, but in our huddled world, we are completely engaged.

We win the coin toss and decide to receive the kickoff. Maybe because of the bad weather, the kick doesn't go far. Terrance catches it at our own thirty-five yard line, breaks a couple tackles, and brings it back to their forty yard line. We have great field position. Because of the giant gusts of wind, Terrance is put to work. I watch from the sidelines as Coach Carlson sends in dives and sweeps. Terrance busts through the line of scrimmage as our line opens huge holes. He puts deceptive moves on the defensive backs and pushes closer and closer to the end zone. On third and two, Terrance takes a handoff from Mike Giffin. As he reaches the first down marker, he seems to relax and stand up. From his blind side, their 250 pound linebacker drives his helmet into the side of Terrance's head, and he goes down limply. Coach Carlson and our trainer sprint out to the field.

From the sideline, all I can see are Coach and the trainer. The entire stadium is quiet, fearing the worst. But, then I see Terrance's legs shift from side to side. This is a good sign. After about ten minutes, they help him to his feet, each grabbing an arm. Terrance looks to be okay, but he wobbles back and forth. They take him to the bench where he complains that he is seeing double and that everything is blurry.

What are we going to do? I think to myself. Losing Terrance means . . . and before I can finish my thought, Coach Carlson looks directly at me and says, "Morris, get in there for Strong. We're going to run 39 pitch. Tell Tommy to get out there on the sweep. If he can get to their outside linebacker, you're in for a touchdown."

"Okay, coach." I start toward the huddle.

Coach Carlson grabs me by the back of my shoulder pads and spins me around to face him. He's calm and confident. "Son, there's no reason you can't do this. If Terrance weren't here, this would be your position." He slaps me on the back of the helmet as I sprint to the huddle.

I meet Mike at the left hash and tell him the play on the way to the huddle on the right hash. I will have the entire wide side of the field to work with. When we get to the huddle, everyone looks freaked out and panicked. Mike shouts, "HEY, WE ARE NOT A TEAM MADE UP OF ONE MAN. QUIT LOOKING LIKE A BUNCH OF LOST BABIES. ARE WE JUST GONNA LIE DOWN CAUSE TERRANCE GOT HURT? WE GOTTA SUCK IT UP."

Everyone in the huddle stands straighter. Mike looks each man in the eyes. "Listen, we're running 39 pitch. Tommy get out on that sweep with Sammy and plant that outside linebacker on his ass. Morris here says he'll do the rest." He shoots a smile in my direction. I nod. "All right, here we go. 39 pitch on two. 39 pitch on two."

We break the huddle and hustle to the line of scrimmage. It's first and ten from the fifteen-yard line. Mike calls the cadence, "Red 44, red 44, set, hut, hut." The ball is snapped. I see the inside linebacker inching up for a blitz. Tommy must see it too because he decides not to pull and pick him up. That puts Sammy on their outside backer. I move in unison with Sammy Jones and catch the pitch in perfect stride. It has been a while since I played tailback. I'm used to following Jack, but my instincts take over. Sammy dives at the knees of the outside linebacker and chop blocks him, which puts me one-on-one with their inside backer. I lower my shoulder and spin off the hit, a drill I have practiced over and over. Their linebacker can't get a hold on me, and I get loose. I sprint toward the end zone, and their safety sprints toward me. I see that the collision will take place around the one-yard line. I lower my shoulder like I am going to run over the safety, but at the last second I jump as high as I can. The safety goes low to meet me and realizes too late that I am airborne. He stands up at the last second. I am five feet in the air. He catches my left foot, and I spin around like a helicopter in the air. The crowd goes silent, unaware that for the moment, they have stopped breathing. I land, safely, in the end zone. Touchdown!! The crowd goes wild, hugging each other and giving high fives. The offensive linemen slap my helmet as they congratulate me, relieved, reassured. Our confidence is back.

After that play the momentum shifts. Terrance has a severe concussion and can't really stand up. I feel bad for him, but I am completely jacked up. I want to run the ball again and again. All I can think about is Jack punishing defenders, and on this day, I don't want to be Walter Payton or Jim Brown, I want to be Jack Thompson.

Coach Carlson probably sees the fire in my eyes, and because of the bad weather, he has no problem giving me the ball. Play after play, I run the ball on counters, sweeps, dives, and traps. Terrance sits out the rest of the game, and I'm in a zone like never before. I anticipate blocks and the moves of the defenders. I touch the chain on my neck under my shoulder pads and absorb the strength from St. Christopher. Like a dragon slayer, on every play I drag two, sometimes three defenders. I tell myself, *No one is going to take down this Cedarville kid.*

By the end of the game, Archbold wants nothing to do with me. I score two more touchdowns, and Mike Giffin throws for another. We win easily 28 to 7.

Archbold's touchdown comes late in the fourth quarter, but they are never really in the game.

Coach Carlson huddles us up in the Baldwin-Wallace locker room and looks over the team. "Men, we learned a lesson about overcoming adversity today." He pauses. "One of our best players went down, and we rose to the challenge. That's what I love about football. It's a lot like life. You will face a lot of adversity in your life, and you're going to have a choice. Do I lie down and feel sorry for myself? Or do I look inside myself and say, 'ain't nothing going to beat me today'?" Coach Kaplan tosses the game ball to Coach Carlson. "Today, a young sophomore rose to that challenge. He stepped up. Game ball goes to Billy Morris. Nice job, son."

My teammates are all looking at me. The crowd noise outside is a muffled hum. But inside that locker room, it's different. It is safe, pure, complete. I miss Cedarville, but I've paved a new road for myself at Bertram. I have found a place beyond just being a part of the team. I have played a respected role, a role that I earned from a summer of hard work and fine-tuning my strengths as a football player.

When we get back to school, it's late. I call Jack's cell phone, but there's no answer. I'll have to wait for tomorrow's paper to see if Cedarville won their semi-final game. I have a restless night trying to sleep and anticipating the possibility of playing Cedarville in the State Championship game.

Chapter 30

November 14 Jack's story

Jack Thompson is playing in the state semifinal football game at Welcome Stadium in Dayton, Ohio. The snow comes down steady, covering the entire field. He gets the ball on a running play to the wide side. His gold number 44 spreads across the front of his royal blue uniform. His torn Kid Rock t-shirt hangs out from under his jersey.

His cleats grab the thin Astroturf as he reads his blocks, eyes widening as he sees a path to the end zone, breathing hard as he turns the corner, squaring his shoulders when he turns up field. He's hoping that someone will come up and hit him, challenge him, so he can lower his shoulder and hurt them, punish them, knock them senseless, make them feel the pain that he feels.

The fans cheer and scream. The stands are loaded with moms, dads, sisters, brothers, the marching band, just about the entire town of Cedarville. The blue and gold colors cover the stands like a canvas. One crazed parent has an air horn that screeches above the noise. The kids shake their milk jugs filled with pennies and scream at the top of their lungs.

Jack bursts through the defense and rambles into the end zone for the touchdown that puts Cedarville on top. After he scores, they form the huddle to go for a two-point conversion. Despite the insanity of the crowd, inside the huddle, it is quiet, almost serene. It is an atmosphere created by trust, discipline, hard work, and love.

In the huddle, the players hold hands. Everybody watches the quarterback, Danny Towers. His eyes scan the team as he says, "Listen, fella's. Let's do this! Punch it in! One time!" He calls the play, "I right 39 sweep on two, I right 39 sweep on two." It's the same play they just ran. The defense knows Jack's getting the ball, and they know that there is nothing they can do to stop him. The offense claps their hands, one time, in unison. They sprint to the line of scrimmage, eyes blazing. They have worked too hard for this opportunity. They taste victory, and they want Jack to be the hero. Danny calls the snap count, "RED 88, RED, SET HUT, HUT."

The ball is snapped. They explode from their stances and fire off the line. They grunt from their hearts, their souls, destroying the team across from them as Danny pitches the ball out to Jack. He is one on one with their free safety. The safety knows that it's his job to come up and make the hit, but he sees who has the ball, pretends to give chase. He wants nothing to do with the force of energy that Jack Thompson has become.

Cedarville heads to the locker room with helmets raised in celebration. In the locker room, Coach Murphy, cheeks filled with chewing tobacco, unshaven, loved by everyone, addresses the team, "Way to go! You boys did something tonight that has never been done before in the history of our school. You'll be playing for a state championship. You know, it's amazing what you can do when you don't care who gets the credit, when you play for your teammates and not just yourself. Don't ever forget that. Keep it locked in your minds, in your hearts." He pauses to catch his breath. He adjusts his hat, takes it all in. "I want each and every one of you to know that I love you guys. You've made this season an amazing experience for the coaches, and the entire town. These are memories you will never forget."

The linebacker coach, Coach Moses, tosses Coach Carlson a football. Carlson looks over the entire team and says, "Time for the game ball."

Each player suggests someone else for the recognition. They are the definition of a team. He tosses the ball, referee style, to Jack. "Thompson. Heck of a game, son."

Jack lowers his head. Danny Towers, Woody Fletcher, and Tombo Howard pound on his shoulder pads. Jack doesn't even smile.

On the way to the bus with Tombo and Woody, Jack sees his dad, leaning up against his '57 Chevy, a car his dad rebuilt with his own hands, from the wheels to the engine to the metallic black paint job. Mr. Thompson has been drinking whiskey from the flask that bulges from the inside pocket of his jeans jacket. "Did you see my boy?" he brags loudly to anyone who will listen. "He was kicking some ass tonight. Not as tough as his old man, but it'll do."

Jack tries to look away from his father before their eyes meet.

"Come over here, boy. What? You embarrassed to be seen with your dad? You too good for your old man? Big football star?" His husky voice stops Jack, unlike any player on the field can.

Parents avoid the scene as they head to their cars. Mr. Thompson walks over to his son and leans into him, putting his arm around him, breathing his whiskey breath into his son's face.

"Come on. I'll give you a ride home. Just put the finishing touches on the Chevy. She's running like a top."

Coach Murphy approaches from the side of the bus. "Mr. Thompson," he begins, "team policy, all athletes ride home on the bus."

Mr. Thompson slurs, "Who do you think you are?"

Coach Murphy, the 6 foot 4 inch, ex-division I football player, looks down at Mr. Thompson and says, "The coach, looking out for my players."

"Yeah, well, I'm his father."

Coach Murphy is close enough that he can smell Mr. Thompson's breath. "Why don't you get a ride home with one of the other parents? I'm sure they'd be happy to drive you home."

"Dad, get a ride with the Howard's. They'll take you," Jack pleads.

"I ain't no charity case." He looks Coach Murphy dead in the eye, sees his resolve, and backs down. "Have it your way, coach."

Mr. Thompson walks toward his car with his keys in hand.

"Dad, don't drive home." Jack pleads with his dad.

Mr. Thompson waves off his son as he slides into his '57 Chevy and starts it up. He revs the engine. It purrs and roars at the same time. Giant snow flakes continue to fall and cover the ground. Mr. Thompson peels out; the back end of his car fishtails—just missing a parked minivan near the exit of the parking lot.

Coach Murphy shakes his head and looks over at Jack. "He'll be alright."

Jack throws his bag on the equipment van and climbs onto the team bus.

Mr. Thompson heads west on route 70 toward 77 south. He squeezes the hard leather ball on the gearshift and pushes on the accelerator, proving to himself that he has built a good car, that he can do something right. The car smoothly switches gears like the well-crafted machine that it is. He smiles, reminds himself that he is a master technician. He curses all the managers that didn't hire him to work at their shops. Morons, he thinks to himself.

His mind drifts to the game and to his son, who is so much the opposite of him. His son is a great athlete: strong, gifted, talented, and well-liked. He loves his son, and at the same time resents him because his son has become everything he never was. He believes he has failed as a father and a husband. Sometimes, he pounds on his son and tells him he's a loser. Damn it, he wants to feel in control of something. He pushes his foot on the accelerator and the speed climbs to 80 miles per hour. He thinks about his wife and the night she left him, how he blamed Jack, knowing it was not his fault.

He pushes down harder on the accelerator, flying by the few cars on Intestate 77 that have braved the slippery, snow covered roads. The needle climbs to 90. He knows he's in danger, but he doesn't care. He's numb. His chest is tight, and he considers whether or not he even has as heart. He thinks to himself, what keeps this bag of bones alive?

That question runs through his mind when the car hits a patch of ice over a bridge. The front left wheel is the first to go. His reaction is slow, almost as if he doesn't want to react. He presses on the brakes, but he's going too fast. His body stiffens knowing that his speed and the ice are a terrible combination. The car begins to spin in circles on the freeway. 180°, 360°. There is a shattering of glass, a loud pop, and the crunching of metal.

The school bus takes a different route back to Cedarville because the bus driver hears on the radio that there is a bad accident on I-77. Jack eases back into his seat, wondering why the bus is taking a different path back to the school. He looks out the side of the bus and thinks about playing in the State Championship. He thinks about his dad, hoping that things will get better for him. He knows he's a good man. He's seen the good side of him when he isn't drinking. But the alcohol has a hold on him. Jack wants his mom to come home. He wants things to be "normal." That word spins in his mind . . . normal. The bus crawls along the slippery road making its way back to Cedarville.

Chapter 31

Saturday November 15th

My alarm clock wakes me at seven a.m. I jump out of bed and make my routine trip to the library. Waiting as always, is Erin; only she is not her usual smiling self. She's crying and her head is buried in her hands. She gives me the paper, but it's not the sports section. It's the front page that reads: *Cedarville's Thompson Dies in Car Accident*. For a moment, I can't catch my breath. My eyes scan to the article:

THE DAYTON FLYER

After Cedarville's big win on Friday night, all the celebrating came to an abrupt end with the news of a deadly car accident. Jim Thompson, father of standout football player Jack Thompson, was pronounced dead at Miami Valley Hospital at 2 a.m. Saturday morning. Partly due to poor weather conditions, and partly due to a high blood alcohol level, Jim Thompson's car slid off Interstate 77 and hit a tree on a stretch of freeway just outside of Exeter. Severe head injuries, reports say, indicate that death was probably on impact. Jim Thompson leaves behind his wife and son.

I can't move. I try to hold back the tears, but they come. I feel like a hole has been seared into my stomach. Erin hugs my head to her stomach and says, "I am so sorry."

I sit there for what seems like an eternity, not wanting to leave Erin's arms, yet I want to run away.

"I need some air," I tell her, and I walk out onto campus like a zombie. I pull the collar of my coat around my neck as I walk into the winter cold trying to figure out what to say to Jack. What could I say? I walk for an hour. The wind is blowing, and the snow is deep. I don't know what else to do. I cry uncontrollably one minute, and then I'm angry as the hell the next.

I go to my dorm. Sean is not there, so I figure now is as good a time as any. I dial Jack's number. It rings about four or five times until a subdued voice answers. "Hello."

"Hey, dude, it's me, Billy. I read the paper. I can't believe it."

Jack is quiet. Then he says, "My old man grabbed me by the jacket and asked me if I wanted to ride with him. I could smell the liquor on his breath. He had his silver flask hanging out of his pocket. I was so pissed off at him. I didn't know what to do. Coach Murphy stepped in and said team policy is that I ride home on the bus. He could tell that my old man was drinking. He even asked my dad to get a ride home with one of the other parents. He would have nothing to do with it. He said he was fine, that he felt great, didn't need anybody's charity. He said nothing could bother him after his son got Cedarville to the State Championship. Parents offered to drive him home. He shouted that he was fine, and he peeled out of the stadium parking lot. I got the news last night when a policeman told me my dad was dead."

"What are you going to do?"

"I don't know what to do. There's a picture of the car in the newspaper today. The thing is crunched up like an accordion. The front of the car is pushed up to the steering wheel. It seems like a bad dream. I keep thinking if I go back to sleep, I'll wake up from the nightmare. The only problem is, I can't sleep."

"Just keep breathing."

"It was bound to happen. He was driving on a suspended license. He shouldn't have been driving."

"What are you going to do?"

"Well, I'm home, sitting on the couch, watching the clock, trying to understand all this," Jack says.

I think about *A Prayer for Owen Meany* and the question Mr. Tanner asked: What does one believe when faith and doubt come into conflict? Is there a God? And how could God do something like this? I didn't know how to answer Jack's question. I say, "You're going to be all right."

I hear a noise in the background at Jack's house.

Jack says, "Hold on one second. Somebody's here."

The phone is quiet, and then I hear a woman's voice, "Honey, are you okay?" I hold my breath and wait.

Jack gets back on the line. "Billy, can I call you back? My mom is here. She's back."

"Man, that's great news," I say. "Call me later."

"I'll call you."

Jack hangs up. I hit the end button on my cell phone and look up at my dorm room ceiling. I exhale a deep breath and feel a sense of relief. Jack's mom is home. I figure maybe there is a God, and he works in very strange ways.

I sit on the edge of my bed and rub my eyes. There are so many questions. Why did this happen? Is Jack going to be okay? What's going to happen now that his mom is home? Will she be okay? Would Jack even consider playing in the State Championship next Friday?

* * *

That night my phone rings. I'm listening to a Neil Young mix CD that Erin made for me. It's Jack, sounding better than when I talked to him last.

"Hey man," I answer.

"Billy, my mom's home. I can't believe it."

"That's awesome."

It seems like Jack wants to tell me everything at once. "She says she never really left. She was always close by but didn't know how to deal with my dad. She keeps apologizing."

"What are you guys going to do?" I ask.

"She has an apartment near downtown Dayton. We'll probably stay there for a while. I can't wait to get out of this house. It's tough being here. It's so depressing." The phone goes silent for a few seconds. Then Jack continues. "You know, I loved my dad. He was a good guy—just didn't know how to make things right. If you really knew him, he was a good guy. I'll never forget the look in his eyes after that last playoff game. I could tell how proud he was of me. He stood up straighter, walked taller. He shook my hand and gave me a hug. He told me he loved me. Can you believe that?"

I remain silent.

"He loved coming to those games. For the last couple of months, it seemed like that was what he lived for. You know, one day, he told me he wanted to get sober, make things right in his life, but he wanted to wait. He said that if he checked into the rehab clinic that he would have to stay there for thirty days. He didn't want to miss any of my games. He said he didn't want to be in some smoky AA meeting while his boy was winning the biggest game of his life. He didn't want to miss any of it. He didn't know what to do or how to make things right again."

Because I feel like I have learned a lot about facing situations that are out of my control, I tell him, "There's nothing you can do to bring your dad back. All you can do is live the best way you know how. Don't make the same mistakes he made. Make him proud. Be the man that he would have wanted you to be. That's the best gift you can give your dad."

"My mom is back, and I want to try to help make things right."

"So the plan is to move into her apartment, start over?"

"Yeah, I guess so." It is then that Jack brings up what I hesitated to address earlier, the state championship football game. Considering everything that's happened, it seems so unimportant. "Hey, can you believe it's going to happen? Can you believe we play you guys in the State Championship game next Saturday night?"

"I know. It's crazy. Never in a million years could I ever have imagined it. When I left three months ago, I wanted nothing more than to play for Cedarville, and now here I am, playing against you guys."

"It will be like the first day of hitting during double sessions, me versus you."

"It'll be a battle, for sure."

"I can't wait."

"Are you actually considering playing?"

"Who me?" Jack asks.

"Yeah, you."

"Are you kidding," he says, "that game . . . that game . . . I wouldn't miss that game for anything in the world. With everything that happened with my dad, it's the one thing keeping me alive."

Chapter 32

November 17th

    Mr. Tanner looks at me as I walk into class. The thought of Jack's father dying is etched on my mind. I can't shake it. I wish that things were as they were before. I wish that things could be right for Jack.

    "Good morning," he says. "Come on in, have a seat. I hope everyone had a good weekend. I know the football team must be excited for the State Championship football game on Friday." There is a rumble of discussion around the room. "We have two more chapters of *A Prayer for Owen Meany*. I trust all of you have done the reading. And most of you are engaged by . . . if nothing else . . . by the voice of Owen." The class laughs at the high-pitched voice of Owen. How for his small size, he was able to have such a huge impact on everyone in his life.

    From the back of the room, Amanda, a field hockey player says, "It's one of those books that you wish never ended." The class chuckles but no one disagrees. I think everyone identifies with the book. It was hard to ignore the voice of Owen and his dilemma. He was a self-proclaimed instrument of God.

    After thinking about Owen, I contemplate the role of God in my life, the role of fate, and the roles of other people in my life. I think about my mom and how her life was so changed by Richard and how that brought me here to Bertram. I think about Cindy and what I thought love was, and then I think about Erin. She has become so much a part of me in such a short time. I look over at her on the other side of the room. Even early on Monday morning, she is super-cute. But on my mind more than anything, is the death of Jack's father.

I stop to talk to Mr. Tanner after class.

"Mr. Morris, what's on your mind?"

"Too much stuff."

He tilts his head to look me in the eye. "What's up?"

"It's just," I pause, "my best friend back home. His dad died this weekend."

Mr. Tanner doesn't seem affected by this news. I guess after two tours in Vietnam, nothing really shocks you. "What happened?" he asks.

"He died on Friday night in a drunk driving accident."

Mr. Tanner looks at me sympathetically. "I have to tell you something," he says, his face getting serious. "When I was in the war, I saw some senseless death. I saw some really bad things, things that still keep me up at night, almost thirty years later. Sometimes people die, and there isn't a thing we can do about it. Sometimes the Lord takes over, and we just have to accept the results. I'm not saying it's right or fair. That's just the way it is."

"I'm just worried about my friend. I don't know how he's going to deal with it."

"Let me tell you a story," he begins. "My best friend and I, we didn't get drafted into Vietnam, we volunteered. We thought we were tough, bad asses, you know. Well nothing, and I mean nothing, can prepare someone for the things that went on in Vietnam. So we end up in the same platoon, best friends full of energy, fearless, going to bust some communist ass. We think we're bad as hell. We strut around the base like we aren't afraid of anything. So we're in country for only two weeks, and we get into this ground attack. Bullets are flying, and I'm ducking for cover. In the middle of the ambush, I look over and see my best friend, Joey Porter, all shot up, laying there with a hole the size of a coconut in his gut. All of a sudden, I'm not so tough anymore. In fact, I'm scared, scared as hell. I want to be home right then. There I am nineteen years old, feeling completely paralyzed."

"What did you do?"

"I just kept praying, praying to just keep breathing. Get Joey out of there; get myself home in one piece. That's why I'm so into religion. When I started praying on the field in Khe Sanh, something happened to me. An energy, a force came to me. It wrapped itself around me, and it told me that there was nothing that was going to hurt me. When I finished my tour, I became very religious. It wasn't any one religion in particular, just a higher power. I combined all of my beliefs to form my own belief system. But something saved me, something that wasn't of this world, something that transcended anything that I had ever known. And that, I have to believe in."

I think I understand what Mr. Tanner is saying. He wants me to have faith, to believe in that higher power, and to use my meditation. But more importantly, I have to realize that the healing and strength are going to come from inside of me, from my own heart. I have to be willing to do the same thing for Jack. I have to help him realize that despite all the things that have happened to him, he's going to be okay. There's no reason he can't get through this.

Mr. Tanner stands up and puts his hand on my shoulder. He looks me directly in the eyes and says, "You and your buddy are going to be all right."

I nod my head.

"If you need anything, you know where you can find me."

I thank him and head to the hallway. Erin is standing there waiting. She walks up to me and without saying anything, she hugs me.

We walk to our next class through the early morning cold. The snow blankets the campus and our footprints are fresh. The wind whips through the center of campus.

"Are you doing okay?" she asks.

"I'll be fine. I'm worried about Jack."

"He's going to be okay. Just be a good friend, and be there for him as much as you can."

"I just wish that all of this never happened."

"I'm really sorry. I want you to know that I'm here for you." Erin puts her arm around me.

"Thanks."

"No problem," she says, trying to lighten the mood.

Her simple gesture makes me feel better.

We get to the music and art building and head to our separate classes. "I'll talk to you later," I say.

"Let me know if you need anything."

My week begins, and the days roll by until Friday when the school has a huge pep rally. Students and teachers cheer as each player is introduced. The small pep band plays a fight song, and the Headmaster addresses the school. He talks about what a great journey the football team has taken the school on and how the team has brought an energy and excitement to the entire Bertram community. But during his speech and in the middle of all that excitement, my mind drifts to Jack.

Chapter 33

November 22nd

The day of the Division IV Ohio State Championship arrives. We load the bus and begin the two and a half hour bus ride to Ohio State University in Columbus, Ohio. Terrance Strong, Mike Giffin, Sammy Jones, and Marcus Tyler sit stone-faced in the back of the bus with their headphones on. This is their second time playing in a state championship game, and it shows. The bus is quiet as we drive through Canton and pass the Pro Football Hall of Fame. The snow falls lightly, dusting the interstate on our way to Columbus.

On the ride down, I think about Jack and playing against my best friend in what will be the biggest football game of my life. I think about the insane journey that started that day in my kitchen. I can still hear my mother's words, "*Billy, come in the kitchen, there's something we need to talk about.*" The day Richard stood behind my mother as she calmly explained that we would be leaving Cedarville. My chest tightens and my heart sinks while I'm on the bus almost four months later. I think about meeting Sean and Erin, and my famous battle with Terrance Strong. I think about Mr. Tanner and the hours I spent meditating, how it helped to transform my life. I think about Jack's father, him pushing Jack around and telling him that he was nothing. I remember back to the baseball game when the police escorted him from the game in their cruiser and how at the end of the game, on the way back to the school, Jack said, "Sometimes I wish he was dead." All I can I think about is that sometimes you have to be careful about what you wish for. The bus rolls onto the Ohio State Campus and down Olentangy Blvd. The bus makes its way through the city on its way to the stadium.

    The silver charter bus pulls into the parking lot that surrounds the Horse Shoe, the stadium of the Ohio State Buckeyes. We file off the bus and the team managers bring out a bag of footballs. We get the lay of the land, jogging around the field as a team with just our warm-ups on. The wind whistles through the east end of the stadium and light rain falls on and off. I partner up with Sean and do some light stretching. Then, we go through our pre-game ritual of putting dirt from our home field in the end zone. Terrance leads the team around the field as we follow him and shout, "Where are you going to put it? Where are you going to put it?" Terrance takes the dirt from a small clay cup and spreads it into the corner of the end zone. We cheer and shout, begin to get ready for the game.

    After throwing and running around the stadium, Coach Carlson shouts, "Let's bring it in." We huddle up around him at the fifty yard line on top of the giant O. "Men, look around you. Take it all in, the opportunity of a lifetime." He pauses and looks around the giant stadium and breathes in the cold winter air. "We're going to the hotel to check in. We'll be there for about four hours, and then we'll come back to the stadium."

    As I exit the stadium, I take a second to look around at the 80,000 empty seats. I imagine what it would be like to play for the Buckeyes in front of a packed crowd on a Saturday afternoon: The Ohio State Buckeyes vs. The Michigan Wolverines. My version of that game is just seven hours away. A steady flurry of snow begins to cover the worn-out artificial turf, mixing with the rain from the night before. Like Coach Carlson, I take a deep breath and savor, taste the moment, and exhale, watching my breath in the cold winter air.

Before I get on the bus, I see a yellow school bus pull into the far end of the parking lot. It's the Cedarville bus. A huge lump sits in my throat. Images of Jack, Coach Murphy, Danny Towers, and Coach Moses flash through my head.

The bus drives to the opposite entrance, and the Cedarville team, led by Coach Murphy, exits the bus. The blue and gold letter jackets file off one by one. I squint to get a glimpse of my buddies until I hear the voice of Coach Carlson. "Morris, let's go."

I turn away and step up on the stairs of the bus, take one last look, and head back to my seat.

Back at the hotel, Sean and I share a room. We throw our bags down and sit on our separate double beds. "How you doing?" I ask.

"Okay, I guess," Sean responds.

"You ready to play?"

"Yeah man, this is what it's about." His response doesn't seem sincere.

"Dude, I'm nervous as hell. I can't believe we're playing Cedarville."

"Yeah, I can't imagine what it would be like playing against your best friends and all. How are you holding up?"

"Man, playing in the Shoe at Ohio State, it's like a dream come true. I just never thought it would be against my old team. Part of me wants to be playing with those guys. Part of me wants to take the field wearing the blue and gold. Cedarville's in my blood."

"I can see wanting to play with your buddies. I don't blame you."

"You know everyone at Bertram is so damn serious. They forget what it's all about, having fun. Jack and those guys work hard and all, but when it comes time to play, they have a blast. They just let it rip. They get fired up. I miss that."

"Yeah, but these guys at Bertram know what it takes. They've been here before."

"I guess you're right, but shouldn't it be fun too?" I ask.

"I wouldn't worry about it." Sean grabs the remote from the table between the two beds and turns on the television to watch ESPN.

I stare at the ceiling and think about the game. Unlike Sean, I'm worried.

* * *

Five o'clock arrives, and we grab our stuff.

We load up the bus as the sun is setting, but by the time we get to the stadium, I notice the blue-black clouds hovering over the Ohio State Campus and the snow turning to a freezing rain. We circle the parking lot and stop by the locker room entrance.

Coach Carlson stands up. He has on a large red coat with a silver eagle on the back. He holds his clipboard in his hand and says, "Men, let's head to the locker room, get suited up, and then we'll go through our warm up."

We walk into the visiting team's locker room. It isn't anything special, big lockers, showers, and chalkboards with X's and O's all over the place, urgent markings from the Division III game that is being played before ours.

After I get dressed and tape my wrists, Coach Kaplan huddles the defense together and goes over the Cedarville offense. Coach Carlson gathers the offense together and goes over how to attack their defense.

Coach Carlson speaks to the entire team together before we take the field. "Men, and I do mean men. I have seen this team become more than just good football players. This team has become a group of hard working and dedicated young men. You guys have applied yourselves like no team I have ever coached. You should all be proud of that. Tonight . . . tonight, let's put it together. Let's win another state championship. Let's make all the folks back at Bertram proud. Make your parents proud. More importantly, make yourself proud. Make this night extraordinary. Be extraordinary. Make it a night you'll never forget. Seniors, this is your time. Be the leaders you know you can be. Let's go! Bring it in!"

The team comes together in the middle of the locker room, and we say the "Our Father." Then we huddle up, and we all put our hands in. The seniors shout, "Let's go. Get it up." Everyone yells and shouts, but I can't help but notice that something is missing. Something is missing.

We fill the tunnel on the opposite side of the stadium from Cedarville. I look out onto the lit up field. As we jog onto the field, I can tell that the rain and freezing temperatures have made the astro-turf slippery, a disadvantage for our outside running game. Our disadvantage will be Cedarville's advantage. The conditions will benefit Jack and his down-hill running style. We are in for one hell of a game.

I glance around the stadium. The fans pack the first two sections of seating all the way around the stadium. There are probably close to 20,000 people. I have never played in front of this many people in my life. The Bertram fans are going crazy. Red and gray colors decorate the stands. The Cedarville fans match their intensity. Royal blue and gold colors are scattered throughout their stands. I catch a glimpse of Cindy. She is wearing a varsity letter jacket. I notice my mom sitting in the Bertram stands with Jack's mother. It's true; she's back. I look around, but I don't see Richard. With so much going on, it's almost impossible to focus on the game.

I catch punts at the fifty-yard-line until I see Jack coming toward me. I jog over to him and without uttering a word, we hug each other. It's good to see my old friend.

"So this is it?" Jack says.

"Yeah, this is what we worked for. I never thought things would play out like this."

"Yeah, well, not much makes sense to me lately."

"You can say that again. I'm sorry about your dad."

Jack looks me in the eye. "Yeah, me too." Jack adjusts his black wristbands over his forearms. "Hey, I gotta get back to the team. Good luck, man."

"Yeah, you too."

He jogs over to his offensive huddle where Coach Murphy sends in plays for the pre-game warm-up.

Coach Kaplan blows his whistle as I jog over to our defensive huddle. The scout offense runs some of Cedarville's plays, which I know by heart. I stand in the back of the huddle and hear someone yelling my name.

"Go get 'em Billy. Go get 'em!"

It's Erin. She waves from the stands, sitting with her friends from the field hockey team. I have to pinch myself to make sure I'm not dreaming: Erin, the state championship football game, my best friend, and the opportunity of a lifetime.

After our fifteen minute warm-up, the captains take the field for the coin toss. Cedarville wins the toss and chooses to receive. We will be on defense first. Coach Carlson brings us together on the sideline. "Come on, men. Let's make it happen. Let's make it happen."

We sprint out to our kick-off positions. We kick the ball deep, and Johnny Phillips runs it to the thirty yard line before Sean brings him down with a solid hit.

Marcus Tyler calls our defensive play. "52 slant, eagle, man. 52 slant, eagle, man."

Cedarville breaks out of their huddle and sprints to the line of scrimmage. The masses of bodies line up against each other. My heart pounds, like it wants to come out of my chest. The linemen get into their three point stances. Jack lines up deep in the backfield, the position that I had earned earlier this summer. I look into his eyes, but they are not his. He has made some kind of sick transformation. On the first play, Jack gets a hand-off over the right tackle. He bursts through the line of scrimmage and blasts right through our biggest defensive lineman, Mel, a 6'5" 295 pound hulk, like he isn't even there. He continues his running assault carrying two or three defenders for another ten yards. He jumps to his feet unphased and sprints back to the huddle.

Play after play, they give Jack the ball on dives sweeps, and off-tackle blasts. With each run, he seems to get stronger, enjoying the physical and violent contact. Jack is fueled by more than the muscles he built up over the summer. He is driven by the death of his father, and he has picked this night to unleash everything that has been bottled up inside him.

His powerful legs break through tackles, and he lowers his shoulder, relentlessly punishing would-be tacklers. The loud speakers echo throughout the stadium. "JACK THOMPSON, THE BALL CARRIER." Cedarville picks up first down after first down. Over and over the voice repeats Jack's name. "JACK THOMPSON, THE BALL CARRIER." And his running assault continues.

Cedarville drives all the way to our two yard line. There's not much talk between the two teams, but there's a lot of talk within the teams. Cedarville's players celebrate with high-fives, as we point fingers and blame each other. Even though it's early in the game, we already feel a sense of urgency. We know that we cannot withstand four quarters of Jack Thompson. On first and goal from the two, they run a tailback trap. Their left guard doubles on the nose. I read trap and shoot into the hole. The play isolates me against Jack. The collision is like an explosion. Jack lowers his shoulder and blasts into me. The pop of the pads travels across the field. He pounds his way through me and steps into the end zone. I roll over and watch as Jack hands the ball to the referee. I steady myself and stand up with wobbly knees and a dazed expression. The speakers boom through the stadium. "TOUCHDOWN CEDARVILLE. JACK THOMPSON ON THE CARRY FOR THE COMETS."

Cedarville kicks the extra point to make the score 7-0.

Our offense is not as effective as the punishing ground game of Cedarville. The freezing rain and the colder nighttime temperatures form a thin layer of ice on the astro-turf. On our first play, a wide sweep to the right, Terrance's feet come out from under him as he slips on the frozen surface. The cold wind and rain prevents us from throwing, and the icy Astroturf doesn't allow our running backs to make sharp cuts.

Our defense begins to come together, and we start gang tackling Jack, who drags two, three, sometimes four defenders. The voice over the loudspeaker continues. "JACK THOMPSON, THE BALL CARRIER."

The second quarter is a back and forth exchange of punts and short drives. With only a few seconds left in the half, Coach Murphy goes into his bag of trick plays. It's a play that I have never seen before. Cedarville runs the hook and ladder with an option thrown into it. These plays usually never work, especially under such horrible conditions. The wide receiver does a twelve yard hook, while the slot back comes behind him, and the other wide receiver trails behind the slot back for the option. We defend the hook and ladder, but it was the option that breaks the play all the way down to our one yard line. Terrance runs down a streaking Woody Fletcher and pushes him out of bounds at the one yard line, but there are still two seconds on the clock.

Both teams huddle up. Everyone in the stadium knows who is going to get the ball. Cedarville breaks the huddle and sprints to the line of scrimmage. We try to get set anticipating Jack getting the ball on a dive or sweep. He only needs one yard for the touchdown.

Danny Towers calls the cadence, "BLUE 22, BLUE 22 SET, HUT, HUT. He sprints to his left to hand off to Jack. Jack plows over the left side of the line pushing the heap of bodies into the end zone. The voice booms over the loudspeakers, and it echoes throughout the stadium. "TOUCHDOWN CEDARVILLE! JACK THOMPSON CARRIES FOR THE TOUCHDOWN."

We are down 14-0 at the half, but our attitudes tell a different story, something like 140-0. We enter the locker room with heads down and spirits broken. There's no explosion from Terrance Strong. The silence in the locker room is deafening.

Terrance comes up to me and says, "Morris, it's like a bad dream. And your boy, Thompson, he's killing us."

I don't even respond. Coach Carlson comes into the locker room and gets down to business. "Men," he begins, "get with your position coaches and let's figure out how to get back in the game." He takes a practical, almost scientific approach to the game: execute, out-smart, and out-play your opponent. His philosophy is simple. But tonight, tonight we need something more. We need a major fire lit under us. And who was I to speak up? For the first fifteen minutes of the half coaches draw up plays and ask players how they can make adjustments. Everyone is listening, but nobody seems emotionally attached, like they want to win.

Before we head out for the second half, Coach Carlson looks around the locker room and looks into the faces of each player on the team. His jaws tighten. "EVERYBODY STOP." Surprised, we all turn and look. His eyes look wild, and for the first time all year, he goes off, "WHAT IS GOING ON? DO YOU GUYS REALIZE THAT THIS IS AN OPPORTUNITY OF A LIFETIME? SENIORS, THIS IS YOUR LAST HIGH SCHOOL FOOTBALL GAME! IN THE ENTIRE STATE OF OHIO, TWO TEAMS MADE IT HERE. TWO TEAMS. YOU HAVE WORKED TOO HARD. YOU HAVE INVESTED TOO MUCH. MAKE SURE YOU DON'T HAVE TO LOOK BACK ON TONIGHT AND WISH THINGS WERE DIFFERENT. YOU CAN MAKE THEM DIFFERENT RIGHT NOW. YOU CAN CHANGE THIS. YOU CAN MAKE THIS THE ENDING THAT YOU WANT. I HAVE ONE THING I WANT TO GET ACROSS TO YOU GUYS RIGHT NOW AND FOR THE REST OF YOUR LIFE. DON'T LIVE YOUR LIFE WITH ANY REGRET. DON'T LIVE YOUR LIFE WISHING THINGS WERE DIFFERENT

WHEN YOU HAVE THE POWER TO MAKE THEM DIFFERENT. NO REGRETS."

The expressions change on the guys' faces. Terrance, Marcus, and some of the offensive and defensive lineman start yelling and screaming and getting each other fired up. His words sink in. Everyone knows that Coach is right.

Coach Carlson must be inspired by his own speech because he decides to make some changes. For one, he takes out senior fullback Sammy Jones and puts me in. "Morris," he says, "show me what you can do."

We take the field for the second half with a different attitude. Cedarville kicks off to Terrance, and he runs the kickoff to the twenty-five yard line. I join the offensive huddle. The linemen have a different look on their faces after the coaches explain that the second half is going to be straight ahead, smash-mouth football. I will be Terrance's lead blocker, and I'm ready for the challenge. Terrance grabs me in the huddle and says, "Hey Morris, you're a bad man. Let's see what you got."

Coach Carlson sends in a succession of inside running plays, plays that do not fit the outside running style of Terrance, but play after play, we pick up first downs. On dive plays, Jack takes me head on more than once. The collisions are violent and nasty, but the offense opens holes. We move down the field. But unlike us, Cedarville doesn't point any fingers. They regroup after each play and bring it even harder on the next play. On each play the offensive and defensive lines fire off the ball, crashing violently into each other. The cold temperature makes me feel each collision down to my bones.

On first and goal from the four yard line, Coach Carlson calls a fullback dive over our right guard. I take the handoff from Mike Giffin and plow over the right side of the line. I dive head first from the two yard line and extend the ball over the goal line. Touchdown!! We kick the extra point to make it 14-7.

I see that my boys from Cedarville aren't sure what hit them. After dominating the entire first half, they find themselves in a battle. Our newly energized defense shuts down their offense. Jack still runs hard and manages to pick up a few first downs, but he does not dominate like he did in the first half.

Late in the third quarter, Terrance breaks a dive play for a 60 yard touchdown to tie the game at 14-14. He gets the handoff and the hole opens up like the parting of the Red Sea. I throw the block on Jack that springs Terrance, knocking him to the ground. Terrance puts a move on Woody Fletcher, that sends Woody airborne, diving to the ground, grabbing at nothing but air. I stand over Jack after my block. Jack gets up after the play, looks at me and says, "Game over."

I'm not sure what Jack means, but I get the sense that I'm about to find out.

Coach Murphy decides to put the game in the hands of his best player—Jack Thompson. Jack gets the ball play after play. The announcer on the loud speaker revisits his mantra. "JACK THOMPSON, THE BALL CARRIER." We pissed off the giant.

Jack powers through our defense, punishing anyone who tries to tackle him. His forearm is cut up, and there is blood on his pants. His eyes narrow. He bounces of tacklers, stumbles, puts his arm down, and like a good wrestler, steadies himself, and continues his running assault. On every play, he gets stronger and stronger.

With two minutes in the game, the score is tied 14-14. Cedarville has the ball on our thirty-five yard line. There's no question that Jack is going to get the ball. Play after play, Jack runs over right tackle, then left tackle. His linemen pick him up and slap him on the helmet as the seconds tick off the clock.

With only twenty-five seconds on the clock, Cedarville has the ball, third down at our six yard line. Danny Towers runs a bootleg to the right after faking to Jack. Our whole defense goes after the fake, except for me. I remember the play from practices with Cedarville and mirror Danny. He breaks the contain of our defensive end. I see his eyes light up as he sees the end zone. He sprints to the corner pylon. I take a good angle and come out of nowhere, running him down at the three yard line, preventing the touchdown. The clock runs down to ten seconds, and Cedarville calls a timeout.

Coach Kaplan jogs from the sideline into our huddle. His voice is hoarse from a full game of yelling instructions from the sidelines. "This is it fellas. This is it. Make it count. They aren't going to kick the field goal from way over on the right hash with the field as slippery as it is. Watch for the sweep. They've been running Thompson up the middle all day. They might try to go outside. Corners we gotta turn the play inside. Linebackers, play inside out. Watch the sweep."

The referee blows his whistle and shouts in a raspy voice, "Let's go, coaches, out of the huddle."

Cedarville breaks the huddle and sprints to the line of scrimmage.

Marcus shouts out the defense, "52 slant lion, eagle, thunder. 52 slant lion, eagle, thunder." I twist my cleats into the turf for better traction.

Danny Towers, his breath turning to smoke in the cold air, calls the cadence, "Red 38, Red 38 set hut, hut." He takes the snap from the center.

I read my guard who pulls hard to his left. It's a sweep to the wide side of the field, just like Coach Kaplan anticipated. I play it perfectly. My course is downhill toward the line of scrimmage and inside out. Jack takes the pitch deep in the backfield. He follows his blocks. His eyes widen as he sees the hole open up, a lane right into the end zone. But he doesn't see me coming. I ram hard into his side. It is a textbook hit, my facemask is on the ball, and I drive against him. Jack tries to break through the tackle, pumping his legs like pistons.

Terrance comes up for run support and blasts into me and Jack. Following Terrance is Marcus. Three powerful bodies hammer in hard against Jack, but we aren't driving against another player. We are driving against an emotion, a will, a desire. Jack refuses to go down. He plants hard on his right foot and explodes with his head down, carrying three of us on his shoulders and back, dragging us, grunting, crying, and refusing to give up. He forces the pile of bodies toward the goal line, down to the three, the two, to the one. When the play comes to an end, with no time on the clock, Jack lies face down on the turf one yard deep in the end zone. Touchdown. 20-14. Cedarville wins. Game over.

Jack is mobbed by his Cedarville teammates. He hands the ball to the referee and jogs over to the sideline in a trance. Our defense is in the end zone, some pounding the turf with their fists, crying.

The next ten minutes are a blur. Both teams wait until Cedarville gets the Championship trophy and Bertram receives the Runner-up trophy. The Cedarville team congratulates each other. We just watch, wishing we were the ones going home with the win.

After the trophy presentation, in the far end zone, Coach Carlson calls the team together. Obviously disappointed, he begins, "Men, I am proud of your effort. After that first half, you could have quit. You could have given up, a good lesson to take with you—never, under any circumstances, give up. I am impressed with your desire not to quit. I believe you all showed a great deal of character out there today. You should be proud. You left it all on the field. Seniors, this is it for you. You guys made one hell of a run. Be proud. Juniors, sophomores, use this game to burn your fire a little brighter as you work in the off-season."

I look around at Terrance Strong, Mike Giffin, Sammy Jones, and Marcus Tyler. There are very real tears, tears of lost opportunity. Even though coach said we left it all on the field, we all know it isn't true. We all know that we didn't play our best game. We failed to make the most of our opportunity. Despite the tears and regret, the team is not overwhelmed by the loss. Maybe we didn't care enough about the game, or maybe we didn't care enough about each other.

I finally understand what Bertram was missing. It wasn't athletic ability or desire to win. Everyone at Bertram had that. What we were missing that Cedarville had was the desire to win for each other. I see what a team can accomplish when they play for each other. It's amazing how much harder you play when you are playing for your teammates and your brothers. Cedarville players genuinely loved each other and were willing to do whatever they had to do to win.

The snow begins to fall again as the teams make their way to the locker room. Jack and I look directly at each other as we meet on the track that surrounds the football field. I extend my hand. In my hand is the St. Christopher medal and Jack's silver chain. I place it in Jack's hand. "You might need this more than me right now." I point to St. Christopher on the medal. "You see, there he is fighting all those dragons."

Jack looks at the medal in his hand and forces a smile. "This game was for my dad," he says. "You know, he just didn't know how to get out of it. He wanted to. I could see it. He loved my mom and me. I wish I could've helped him."

"You did what you could."

"Yeah, well, none of this makes any sense."

I look over into the stands and see my mom sitting with Jack's mom.

"I wonder where Richard is?" I say.

Jack responds, "My mom said things didn't work out. She says your mom might be moving back to Cedarville. What do you think about that?"

"I don't know," I say stunned.

"Maybe you can come back to Cedarville and be with the boys?"

"Believe me," I begin, "it hasn't been easy for me, either. Being away from you guys has been brutal. All season long, I wished I was playing with you guys."

Jack says, "Coach Murphy told us that no matter what happened tonight, that we should know that he loves us, and this has been one of the most amazing things in his life. I would do anything for him."

"I know what you mean."

"We'd love to have you back."

"Yeah, it would be good to be back, but it looks like everyone has pretty much moved on."

"What do you mean?"

"I see Cindy got herself a new boyfriend," I say.

"Yeah, after you broke up with her she started dating Danny. I don't think she really likes him. He's just someone to hang out with. She misses you. She tells me all the time."

I think about Erin and wonder what will happen.

Jack says, "It looks like either way, you can't lose. You have a great school at Bertram, but you got good friends in Cedarville."

"I guess it all depends on what my mom decides to do. You know it's funny, I've met some amazing people here." I think about Erin, Sean, and Mr. Tanner.

"No kidding?" Jack says. "Well, I'd love to see you come back. Hey, I gotta get back with the team. Call me and let me know what's happening with you and your mom." We give each other a hug.

"Hey man, great game."

"Yeah, you too."

Jack turns with his helmet in hand and jogs back to the locker room.

I turn and head toward the locker room. Erin is waiting by the fence that surrounds the track. She is bundled up in her winter hat, scarf, and gloves.

She leans over and gives me a big hug. "Hey, you guys played hard. I've never seen two teams play as hard as you guys played tonight. It was a great game."

What Erin said is nice, but I know that sometimes playing well isn't enough. I wanted to win that State Championship in the worst way. I wanted to say that we were the best team in the state. I shrug my shoulders and see that Erin understands so much more about things than I do. She understands that football is just that, a game. And yet it's not just about the game. It's the willingness to put everything you've got into something. Even though we lost, I know that I'm a better person for having had the experience. During the playoffs, we played against the best athletes in the state. We competed like warriors and proved that we belonged. We could play with anybody. I realize that Cedarville was not necessarily the better team. Maybe if we played them on another night, under different circumstances, we might've won the game.

But Cedarville brought something to that stadium tonight, and it was in Jack Thompson's heart. It was his fearlessness that said: *Anything you can dish out won't hurt me be because I've been through something no one should have to go through in a lifetime. Keep trying to knock me down, because I'm coming back every play. And I'm coming back harder each time.*

I hug Erin and thank her for coming to the game. Before I reach the locker room, I see Mr. Tanner. "Mr. Morris, that was one hell of a game. You guys played tough. I am really proud of you. You've got nothing to be ashamed of. Keep your head up, son."

Mr. Tanner has a look of true pride, and his words mean everything to me.

"Thanks, Mr. Tanner." I say and extend my hand.

Tanner shakes my hand and pats me on the back. "I'll catch up with you back at school," he says as he slips back into the crowd.

I glance over and see my mother approaching me with tears in her eyes. She doesn't even let me speak. "I am so sorry," she begins, "I thought what I was doing was best for everyone. Sometimes, people make mistakes. I wish I could take it all back."

"Mom, I understand."

My mother stops me again, "I want to make things right. I want to make things good again."

"Where do we go from here?"

"Well, Jack's mom and I talked about Jack finishing his semester at Cedarville, and then maybe him going to Bertram."

I can't believe it, the best of both worlds, a great school with Jack and Erin.

"So what happened to Richard?" I ask.

"We didn't see eye to eye on a lot of things."

"I'll talk to you when I get back to school." We hug, and I start walking toward the locker room. Most of the fans have cleared out of the stadium.

Chapter 34

On the bus ride back to Bertram, I slide down in my seat and put my headphones on. My mind starts to recall the last five months of my life. I think about the trip with Cindy and her family to Lake Michigan, and Jack's touchdown that won Cedarville a State Championship.

I look out the window of the bus onto the highway into the dark night. As the snow comes down, I think about how in the last five months, I discovered more than just who I am and where I was going. I discovered the real importance of never giving up. From Mr. Tanner, I learned compassion and gained an appreciation for books and my education. From the death of Jack's father, I learned that bad things happen sometimes, and there's nothing that we can do about it. From Erin, I learned that people come into our lives for a reason. But most importantly, from Jack, I learned to treasure my friendships—because a best friend can be the most important thing in the world.

Riding on the bus, I think that my sophomore football season will be one I will never forget. What I thought was going to be the worst experience of my life became my greatest experience yet. I feel that in many ways while living in Cedarville, I was going about my small-town-business in my small-town-way. Going to Bertram and meeting people like Sean, Terrance,

Mr. Tanner, and especially Erin, let me see the world in a totally new way. I gained an appreciation for the roles people play in my life.

    I think about all the people that have affected my life. I discovered that each person I meet, if it's only for a minute, a year, or a lifetime, has been sent to me for a reason.

Chapter 35

December—August

    Bertram was excited to find out that Jack wanted to transfer. And after his State Championship performance, they offered him scholarships to help pay for his full tuition. Jack saw it as a great opportunity to get away from Cedarville.

    My mom and I have reconciled. I finally realized that she was doing what she truly believed to be in my best interest. She had gone into her savings fund to pay for tuition at Bertram. My mother talked to the Admissions Director and was able to get some scholarship money, too. He agreed after learning that my mother would not be able to afford two more years at Bertram. My mom did happen to find a new job as a secretary for an accounting firm. She says it's one hundred times better than that factory.

    Erin came down to Cedarville from Columbus for New Year's Eve. She and my mom hit it off right away. I guess I can't imagine anyone not liking Erin. Jack, Erin, and I went to Mills Diner and went to a late movie. We hung out like three best friends.

    In the winter, I played on the junior varsity basketball team. I got some varsity playing time. That senior class was loaded with great athletes. We ended up losing in the state quarter-finals.

I ran track for Bertram in the spring, and Jack, after transferring during winter break, pitched for their varsity baseball team. Jack became immediately popular at Bertram. Everyone liked him. He has that kind of personality. He even met and started to hang out with one of Erin's best friends from the field hockey team.

And before I knew it, our sophomore year was over.

That summer, Jack and I ran workouts at Bertram's track, preparing for our junior year. Bertram would be losing one of its best senior classes ever. Terrance was going to play for Joe Paterno at Penn State. Four other seniors would play at Division I schools. Jack and I knew that we had our work cut out for us, but we knew that two best friends together could do anything.

Sitting on the football field, surrounded by the track after a workout, Jack gets this distant look. I know he's thinking about his dad and how things could have been different. It was just one of those things that you wish with all your heart hadn't happened.

"You know," Jack says as he stretches his legs. "My dad sent a letter before he died. He had to serve that weekend in jail for his first D.U.I. I guess he had to write a letter home. Well, he wrote to me."

"Yeah, so what did he say?"

Jack pulls his bag toward him. "You want to read it?"

"Sure, if it's okay with you."

Jack reaches into his bag and pulls out the letter. The letter is something that he carries with him. He carefully unfolds the letter, looks it over, and reads through it. He pauses for a moment, probably considering whether or not he wants to share something so personal. Then, he hands me the letter and the envelope.

I take the envelope. It is mailed from the county jail. I examine the letter, and then I look up at Jack. He nods his head, showing that it's okay, that he wants me to read it. The writing is messy, but I do my best to make out what it says. I begin to read:

Jack,

Part of what I gotta do here is that I have to write this letter to someone in my family. So I picked you. I think I've ruined just about every relationship in my life. For some reason, you've stuck by me. I don't know why, but you have. I wanted to tell you a story, something that I've never told you before. You know your grandpa used to drink a lot. He used to beat me up pretty good when I was a kid. He would come home drunk from the bar and take off his leather belt. When I got older and bigger, and he was drunk, I used to throw him out of the house. Your grandma didn't know what to do, so I would just push him out onto the front yard and lock the door. While I was growing up, I told myself I didn't want to be like my dad. Well, fifteen years later, I failed to become something else, I became exactly like him. I guess what I'm trying to say is that I don't want you to be like me. You got so much ability. I see you running that ball. I see you playing football and baseball and I see how you carry yourself. I don't know how you done so good. It's real hard for me to say things like this, but I just want you to know that I'm real proud of you. I know I'm not real good at showing it. I wish I didn't mess everything up. I been trying to get my life back in order. Believe me, I been trying. If there's one thing I would want you for you to do son is to be something better than me. My life isn't what I thought it would be. But you have a chance to make your life something better, something good. That's what I want for you.

Love, Dad

I look over at Jack, who is wiping the tears from his eyes.
"He loved you," I say.
"Why did it have to happen this way?" Jack asks.
I stand up and reach down to give Jack a lift. "It's a chance."
"A chance to do what?" We start walking off the field.

"To open your eyes, man. It's a chance to wake up, a chance to break the cycle."

"Break the cycle?" Jack asks.

"Yeah, you have a chance to make your life different from your dad's. You don't have to end up like him. You don't have to make the same mistakes." I hand the letter and the envelope to Jack.

He takes the letter, folds it, and carefully puts it back in the envelope. He puts it back in his bag and looks at me, saying, "How do I do that? My dad is what I know."

"No man, you're not like him. You're a winner, and a hard worker. Plus, you've had so many good people around you, so many good role models, Coach Murphy, Coach Moses. And now you have the people here at Bertram, Coach Carlson, and Mr. Tanner."

"But why did it have to happen this way?" Jack asks.

I think back to my conversation with Mr. Tanner after I found out about Jack's father. I think about what he said about losing his best friend in Vietnam. I look at my best friend and say, "Sometimes bad things happen, and there isn't anything we can do about it."

"So how do I get through it?" Jack asks.

I look at my best friend and say, "Your friends. Somebody once told me, a best friend could be the most important thing in the world."